Book 2 ❖ J...

HITCHED

Carol Duerksen & Maynard Knepp

Illustrations by Susan Bartel

Hitched
Book 2 — Jonas Series
Copyright © 1996 by WillowSpring Downs

Second Printing, 1999

Printed in the United States of America

Cover and Story Illustrations by Susan Bartel
Page design & layout by Good Shepherd Publications
Hillsboro, Kansas

THE DANCE, words and music by Tony Arata
(C) 1989 Morganactive Songs, Inc.
All Rights Reserved   Used by Permission
WARNER BROS. PUBLICATIONS U.S. INC., Miami, FL. 33014

This story is a fictional account of an Amish family. Names,
characters, places and incidents are either imaginary or are used
fictitiously, and their resemblance, if any, to real persons, living
or dead, is purely coincidental.

Library of Congress Catalog Number 96-60896
ISBN 0-9648525-1-9

Contents

Chapter 1

Tickets

"**H**ey, hot stuff, you wanna sit with me at the *singin'* tonight?" Jonas Bontrager's blue eyes flirted with the dark brown eyes in Sue Ann Eash's sun-kissed face. She sure is lookin' good tonight, Jonas thought to himself. Not that that's anything new.

"If you mean it's hot and sticky out here, and it's going to be worse inside the house, then sure, I'll sit by you," Sue Ann played along.

"That's exactly what I meant," Jonas chuckled. "By the way, you been laying out in the sun, or how'd you get so tan? I thought you were always inside, working at that restaurant, making lots of tips from flirting with the construction guys."

"Well, after I leave work at 3:00, I ride my bike down to the river, put on my hot pink bikini, and lay out for a couple of hours. You mean you've never seen me there?"

"You've got to be kidding!" Jonas couldn't believe he hadn't heard about this from the guys—from someone! "You *are* kidding?"

Sue Ann just smiled, her eyes dancing mischievously.

"Let me see your tan lines then!"

"Not now, Jonas! It's time to go in!"

Along with thirty-some other Amish teenagers, Jonas and Sue Ann began moving toward the large white farmhouse—the home Sue Ann lived in with her parents, brothers, and sisters. The hot July Sunday evening was typical for Kansas—still 90 degrees at 7:00 p.m. Only this evening there wasn't even a breeze to move the air around. Without the modern conveniences of air-conditioning or electric fans, the house would feel like an oven.

Chapter 1

It reminded Jonas of a very similar Sunday evening—why, it happened to be exactly two years ago. It was the first time he sat with Sue Ann at a singing. But that wasn't what made the evening memorable. It'd been the first singing after Enos was killed.

Enos! His good friend, wild and crazy Enos. Always pushing the edge, whether with his car, his drinking, or his life in general. The church ministers said he had it coming, Enos did. But it wasn't Enos's fault he got caught in the crossfire between rival gang members in Vicksburg. The Amish young folks had just been there to have a good time—see the 4th of July fireworks and then go to the river for a party. And then the gunshots, and Enos lying in a pool of blood on the concrete....

Jonas shook his head, trying to bring himself back to reality. By now, he and Sue Ann and the other young people were seated on long, gray, backless benches in the house. Sue Ann's father, Cris, stood in the center of the room and announced, in the native Pennsylvania Dutch dialect they spoke, "Let's pray."

A long silence followed, broken finally by Cris clearing his throat. "Welcome to our home," he said. "We have plenty of food, and look forward to your singing afterwards."

Platters of ham and cheese sandwiches, bowls of Jell-O, and chips began making their way down the tables. Jonas leaned toward Sue Ann and said quietly, "You know what happened two years ago?"

Sue Ann's eyes clouded. "Yeah, Enos was killed. Doesn't seem like that long."

"Nope. I can still see him there on the ground."

"It was awful," Sue Ann looked away, and Jonas knew she didn't want to talk about it any more. Neither did he.

After the meal was over and the plates cleared away, Jonas helped hand out the songbooks. At 19, Jonas was one of the older guys in attendance. Sue Ann was 21, and her main reason for being there was out of respect for her parents, because it was being held at their home. Usually, the young folks at singings were the 16- to 18-year-olds, who were still somewhat new at "running around," and the couples who were going steady and thinking about joining church and getting married. Jonas, Sue Ann, and a few others didn't fit in either category. Having experienced several years of being "on the loose," they were enjoying what the world had to offer, and didn't feel particularly committed to anything Amish.

Some of the songs the young people sang that evening were familiar gospel songs and choruses. Others leaned more toward the sing-song chanting style of the Amish church. All were done a cappella.

Jonas felt the sweat collecting on his back, and he wiped his forehead with his hand. He caught Sue Ann's eye as they sang. "Now look who's the hot one!" she kidded between verses.

❖ ❖ ❖

Along with the other Amish young folks, Jonas stayed at Sue Ann's farm late into the night after the singing. A stock pond in the pasture provided the perfect setting for the youth to hang out, listen to music on their boom boxes, roast marshmallows, play cards, and talk. Although the girls had worn traditional Amish dresses to the singing, they'd changed quickly to shorts and cool tops for the rest of the evening. Most of the guys had given up their barn-door pants when they turned 16, and wore blue jeans and shirts to the singing. Their parents weren't thrilled about it, but they were thankful the kids went to the singing at all.

Sometime around 2:00 a.m., Jonas decided to head home. He untied Lightning, his big bay gelding, from the fence where he'd been standing since Jonas arrived for the singing earlier that evening. Jonas climbed into the open single-seat buggy behind his horse and turned him down the road toward home. It didn't take long before Jonas's head began to nod, and his hands relaxed their grip on the reins. Jonas woke briefly to tie the reins loosely to his leg, then allowed himself the luxury of sleep. Lightning knew his way home.

Chapter
1

❖ ❖ ❖

Jonas hated Monday mornings. He hated how he felt. He hated how his parents, Fred and Esther, looked at him with those "When will you ever learn?" glances. He hated how his younger brothers and sisters were full of energy and fun at 5:00 in the morning, and he could barely drag himself out of bed.

But drag he did, and mumbled a good-bye as he headed out the door. Jonas could barely see as he walked across the farmyard in the pre-dawn darkness. Something rubbed against his ankle, and he stooped down to pick up a huge reddish-orange tomcat. "Hey, Red," he said. "How're you doin', big guy?"

Red responded loudly, and Jonas had to smile. Red always did like to talk. "Gotta get to work," Jonas said, dropping the cat gently to the ground. "I'll see ya later."

Jonas had reached the row of trees bordering the farmstead on the north. Parked under the trees was an old white 1967 Ford pickup. It belonged to Harlan Schmidt, Jonas's boss. Harlan let Jonas use it to drive to and from work. He pulled open the rusted door and slid onto the torn seat. Moments later, he roared through the farmyard, chickens and cats scattering in every direction.

It was five miles into Wellsford, and then another three miles north to the Schmidt dairy. Jonas had been working for Harlan ever since he turned 16. Amish tradition called for all of his earnings to go to his father, and they did. Except for the bonuses Harlan gave him—like a calf every few months. Jonas was amassing quite the little herd at Harlan's—something his father didn't know about. He didn't need to know, Jonas reasoned. This was his savings account. Besides, he earned it. Harlan kept telling him what a good hired hand he was.

"Morning, Jonas!" a bright female voice greeted the lanky, muscular young man as he opened the pickup door and stepped out. "How was your weekend?"

Debbie. Ever-bubbly, ever-friendly, ever-sweet Debbie. They were the same age, and he'd known her since he started working there. They'd even dated for awhile. Until Enos got killed.

"Do you *remember* your weekend?" Debbie teased, falling in stride with Jonas as he walked toward the dairy barn.

"Sure I remember my weekend," Jonas retorted, his voice more tired than angry. "I'm just not quite awake yet. Give me some time."

"No problem. I'll be feeding the calves. Come see me when you get done milking."

Yeah, yeah, Jonas thought, trudging into the barn. It wasn't that he didn't like Debbie. In fact, he liked her a lot. Always had. At one point, he'd wondered if he was in love with her. Which would have broken his parents' hearts, they kept reminding him. Anyway, when Enos was killed, the ministers had really poured it on at the funeral. If you aren't saved, if you wander away from the teachings of your parents and the church, if you experiment with worldly things ... ah, then who knows what will happen to you. Judgment day is coming! It was downright scary stuff. Enough at the time, at least, for him to reconsider his relationship with Debbie and stop dating her.

She'd said she understood. Maybe she did, maybe she didn't. They were still good friends, but she was away at college now, except for the summers.

Jonas moved down the two rows of big black and white Holsteins, washing their teats, putting milkers on, then taking them off and chasing the cows out. He brought sixteen more into the dairy barn and repeated the process. Two hours later, all eighty had been milked. He washed down the milking parlor with a hose and disinfectant, and was hanging up the hose when Debbie walked in.

"Need help in here?" she asked. "You're usually done before I am. But then, this *is* Monday morning," she teased again. "By the way, Mom says she wants to talk to you."

Chapter 1

Lynne wanted to talk to him? What could she want?

"I haven't told Debbie about this," Lynne explained as Jonas stood just inside the kitchen door a few minutes later. "I sent in money for tickets to the Garth Brooks' concert, and our envelope was picked in the drawing! We got four tickets, and Harlan and I were wondering if you'd like the other two."

"Well, yeah, wow, sure! Really? You got tickets!!??"

"Uh-huh. You can have two. And Jonas, it's up to you who you take, okay? They're your tickets to do with as you please."

"Okay! Thanks! Can I pay you for them?"

"Don't bother. Consider it part of your bonus this month."

"Gee, thanks, Lynne! Thanks a lot!"

❖ ❖ ❖

Jonas lay awake that night in the hot upstairs bedroom he shared with his three brothers. Fourteen-year-old David should have been in the same bed with him, but he'd opted for the floor. It was just too hot. Orie, 13, and Robert, 10, were asleep in their underwear in the other bed.

Jonas got up and tiptoed to the door and down the hall. His sisters shared another room. He could see 16-year-old Roseanne sitting at her desk, writing in her diary under the light of a small lantern. Robert's twin, Rebecca, was sleeping.

"Roseanne!" Jonas whispered.

"What?" she asked, looking up while instinctively covering the diary page.

"I need to talk to you."

"Okay. Where?"

"On the porch."

Roseanne blew her lantern out and grabbed a small flashlight. They tiptoed past their parents' bedroom, down the creaky stairs, and out to the screened-in porch. The south breeze felt good.

"Lynne gave me two tickets to Garth Brooks today," Jonas said, sitting down and leaning against the wall.

"And you're wondering if I want to go along?" Roseanne answered in the dark from the porch swing.

"No stupid, not quite," Jonas said, almost wondering why he was talking to his sister about this in the first place. He certainly wouldn't have a year ago. But now that she was 16 and running with the young folks, they'd grown closer. They were beginning to share some common feelings and experiences.

"I was just kidding. So what's the problem?" Roseanne asked.

"I'm sure Harlan and Lynne expect me to take Debbie. But you know who's the absolute biggest Garth Brooks fan?"

"Let me guess. Sue Ann."

"Right."

"So you have to decide who to take."

"You got it."

"Good luck, big brother."

"Come on, Roseanne, help me out!"

"Look, if you do what I say and then you regret it, you'll blame me."

"Probably."

"So, good luck, big brother."

"Well, what would you do?"

"I'd take me."

"A lot of help you are."

"Okay, I'd take Sue Ann."

"And sit with her next to the Schmidts? That's crazy!"

"Okay, I'd take Debbie."

"But Sue Ann would die for this chance. And I wouldn't mind

dying there with her."
"When's the concert?"
"August 4."
"I'll keep that evening open."
"Dream on, sister, dream on."

Chapter
1

Chapter 2

The Dance

Why do you have to make things so hard for yourself? Jonas
scolded himself as he roared off the Schmidt's farmyard
the afternoon of August 4. He shifted the old white pickup into
fourth gear and headed toward Wellsford.

The easy thing would have been to ask Debbie. Harlan and
Lynne had offered to take him and his date along to the Garth
Brooks concert so they would have been a happy foursome. But he
couldn't accept their invitation, because he wasn't taking their
daughter. Instead, he'd asked if he could borrow the pickup for
the evening, and said he'd see them at the concert.

Jonas cruised down Wellsford's Main Street, checking the
time on the bank clock sign. Almost 3:00. Sue Ann would be getting off work in a few minutes. He continued down Main to the
end of the business section and turned left into the parking lot of
The Deutschland Restaurant.

Before long, Sue Ann emerged from the restaurant and ran
lightly toward the pickup.

"You been waiting long?" she asked, sliding a small suitcase
onto the seat between them before jumping up into the cab.

"Just got here," Jonas smiled back. "You ready to ride this ol'
junker into Vicksburg?"

"You couldn't manage anything with air-conditioning?" Sue
Ann faked a frown. "What kind of date is this? It is so hot!" she
fanned herself with her skirt. The action didn't escape Jonas's

appreciative eye.

"Sorry, it was the best I could do," he apologized. "You can change into cooler clothes in Vicksburg."

"You know, I haven't been back to the Vicksburg stadium since Enos was killed," Sue Ann grew serious.

"Me neither. It's going to be strange. I hear they've really spruced up their security since then," he said, knowing Sue Ann's queasiness matched his own.

Chapter
2

Jonas and Sue Ann had always found it easy to talk with each other, and the hour-long drive into the city passed quickly, even in the 100-degree heat.

"Let's stop at the Western store on the way in," Sue Ann said as they reached the outskirts of Vicksburg.

"Okay," Jonas said, a question in his voice. "You buying yourself some boots or something?"

"You'll see."

❖ ❖ ❖

"I still don't know why you did this," Jonas said thirty minutes later. He ducked as he slid into the pickup, then adjusted the black suede cowboy hat over his thick blond hair. He glanced in the rearview mirror and shook his head.

"I got paid today, and I wanted to thank you for taking me to the concert," Sue Ann grinned. "Plus, I've always wondered how you'd look in a black cowboy hat. Now I know."

Jonas was too embarrassed to ask her to finish the thought, but he was dying to hear it. His eyes asked the question, and Sue Ann's smile broadened even more.

"Best-looking Amish cowboy I ever did see."

❖ ❖ ❖

The next stop for the old pickup and its youthful couple was McDonald's. Sue Ann disappeared into the women's restroom with her suitcase, and Jonas took a brown paper bag he'd brought along into the men's restroom. It didn't take him long to change from his work clothes into a stiff pair of almost-new blue jeans and a short-sleeved, western-cut shirt. The blue plaid shirt highlighted the blue in his eyes; his muscular arms sported the usual farmer's tan. Pulling the new hat down low over his eyes, he surveyed himself in the mirror. She'd said he looked good. A rush swept through his body. This was going to be an awesome evening!

Chapter 2

Jonas left the room and waited for Sue Ann. When she finally came out, he almost whistled out loud. He'd seen these transformations many times before—Amish girls going into a room wearing their conservative homemade dresses, hair up behind prim white caps, and moments later, they'd emerge looking, for all the world, just like "the world." Long, shiny hair cascaded down their backs. Cute blouses or T-shirts and jeans or shorts revealed youthful bodies that caught the eyes of more than just Amish guys.

Yes, he'd seen these transformations before, but this one took his breath away. At 21, Sue Ann was a stunning young woman. Her dark brown hair framed a no-make-up-needed face, and hung down her back. Thick, dark lashes outlined chocolate brown expressive eyes—eyes that could dance with fun or touch with tenderness. Jonas didn't know where her tan lines were, and he didn't really care. The arms and legs he saw were smooth, brown, beautiful. He smiled, tipped his hat, and said, "Excuse me, ma'am, but I'm fixin' to attend the Garth Brooks concert. If you don't have any other plans, it'd be my pleasure to have you accompany me."

"Don't mind if I do, cowboy," Sue Ann responded, her gaze sweeping Jonas from head to toe, her eyes registering approval. "You have some fancy wheels waiting outside, I assume?"

"Yes ma'am. But first I thought we'd have a gourmet meal at this here restaurant. Are you hungry?" Jonas gestured toward McDonald's menu. "Take your pick. I feel rich tonight."

Laughing and joking, the Amish young people ate Big Macs and then got back into the '67 Ford pickup. This time, Sue Ann's suitcase occupied the space next to the passenger door.

❖ ❖ ❖

Jonas and Sue Ann found their seats in the large stadium, and
Harlan and Lynne arrived shortly thereafter. Jonas had been
apprehensive about sitting with them, knowing they might be disappointed he hadn't chosen Debbie. After the initial introductions
were out of the way, Lynne proved herself good to her word. She'd
told Jonas it was up to him who he brought, and if she was upset
that he hadn't chosen her daughter, she didn't show it. Lynne and
Sue Ann exchanged small talk for a few minutes, and then the couples turned their attention to each other and the concert.

Sue Ann loved Garth Brooks's music. She knew the words to
almost every song he sang that night. Although the Amish religion didn't allow for cars, telephones, or electricity, she'd owned a
battery-operated CD player since she was 16. Most of the young
folks did. Guys had them in their buggies. Girls listened to them
in their rooms. Along with her CD player, Sue Ann had a large
poster of Garth in her room, a Garth T-shirt, and country music
magazines that she read by lantern light. She knew most of the
country artists and what they sang.

Watching her at the concert, Jonas could see Sue Ann was in
seventh heaven—singing along with most of the songs, soaking
up the atmosphere, her eyes shining with happiness. Without a
doubt, he'd made the right choice.

"Oh, this one is still the absolute best!" Sue Ann enthused to
Jonas as the band led into another song. "'The Dance.' Listen to
these words, Jonas!"

He'd heard the song before. He listened again. And when
Garth sang the chorus, Jonas reached for Sue Ann's hand.

I'm glad I didn't know
the way it all would end
the way it all would go,

Garth's voice declared, and continued,

Our lives are better left to chance
I could have missed the pain
But I'd have had to miss the dance.

A beautiful song. A beautiful woman beside him. A beautiful evening. It doesn't get any better than this, Jonas figured.

❖ ❖ ❖

"They seem like nice people," Sue Ann said as she and Jonas sat in the pickup, waiting their turn to move in the crammed parking lot.

"They are," Jonas answered. "They've been very good to work for. You know what Harlan's doing for me? He's giving me a calf every few months. Sort of as a bonus, 'cause he knows all my money goes to Dad."

"I'd say he's being *very good* to you."

"You know it. I've been selling the bull calves and saving the money. The heifers are staying at his farm. Two of them are old enough to breed now, so I've got a start on a small dairy herd of my own."

"Why's he doing this for you?"

Jonas didn't answer immediately. When he did, Sue Ann could barely hear him over the rumbling of the old truck. "He says it's because I'm a good hired hand and he wants to reward that."

Deep in thought, Sue Ann paused before she spoke again. "Do you think it has anything to do with them wishing you'd end up in their family? As in marrying their daughter someday?"

"I don't know. They've sure never said that."

"Actions speak louder than words, Jonas," Sue Ann paused again, then continued. "Are you tempted to leave? I mean, for good?"

They were finally out of the parking lot, and Jonas was giving most of his attention to driving in the heavy after-concert traffic. He'd never done this before, and it made him more than just a little nervous.

"Anybody coming in the right lane?" he asked, flipping on the turn signal, which didn't work. Sue Ann peered through the window behind her, then gave him the go ahead. "But do it fast," she added.

Jonas felt slightly better once they got onto the freeway. There he could pick a lane and just stay in it. Several miles down the interstate, he questioned, "What were we talking about? Did you ask me something?"

"I asked if you've thought about not being Amish."

"Not be Amish? Yeah, there're times when I wonder about that," Jonas admitted. "Like tonight. What was so wrong with us driving into Vicksburg to see a concert? Where in the Bible does it say that's wrong?"

"I don't know. I do know I'll miss being able to listen to music if I join."

"*If* you join? Are you considering not going back?" Jonas's mind flashed back three years, when Sue Ann was seriously dating Sam. Everybody had them almost married off already. But when Sam made it clear he wasn't going to be Amish, Sue Ann broke it off. "We were born Amish, and that's what we are meant to be. It's all we know." Those had been Sue Ann's words when she told Jonas about the breakup. He'd never been able to get those words out of his mind.

"No, not really. I had that chance when I was with Sam. I'm sure I'll end up joining."

"Some people would say 'You're 21! What are you waiting for?'" Jonas's voice teased lightly.

"'Some people' would say that? Are you 'some people'? And what about you? Why aren't you taking catechism and getting ready to join?"

Chapter
2

"And give up my new cowboy hat?" Jonas smiled at the young woman beside him. "Would you really want me to do that?"

"Never," Sue Ann responded quietly. Something about the tone in her voice spurred a warm rush through Jonas. The electricity between the two Amish young people filled the forbidden truck, and when Sue Ann snuggled closer and put her arm around his shoulders, Jonas melted.

The twosome stopped in Wellsford to get Sue Ann's bicycle, which she'd ridden to work and left at the restaurant when Jonas picked her up. While there, Sue Ann slipped her dress over her shorts and blouse, and hiked her long hair back up under her covering. Jonas waited for the reverse transformation to be completed, then opened his door for Sue Ann to slide into the truck again. As he turned on the ignition, the truck's radio sputtered, then the DJ's voice filled the cab, "And now, for all you Garth fans who made it to his concert tonight, and for those who are wishing they had ... 'The Dance.'"

The parking lot of The Deutschland Restaurant sat deserted at 1:00 a.m. A solitary old Ford truck waited to leave... waited while the young couple inside held each other close, and Garth Brooks sang through a crackly radio. Sometime near the end of the song, Jonas unwrapped his arms from Sue Ann. Holding her shoulders gently, he tilted his head slightly so the hat wouldn't get in the way. His lips found hers softly, smoothly. Her response was what dreams are made of, he thought, his heart pounding crazily. Then, tenderly teasing, Sue Ann pulled away, caressed his mouth with her fingertips, and said, "I always did wonder how good an Amish cowboy could kiss. Now I know."

Chapter 3
The Pain

Jonas parked the Schmidt pickup about a fourth of a mile from his home along a lane leading into a field, and began walking. No way was he going to roar onto the yard with the truck at 1:30 in the morning. Talk about asking for trouble....

But trouble awaited him—he could see it from a distance. A lantern light shone brightly in the living room. One or both of his parents was waiting up for him.

He couldn't believe it. He was used to leaving for entire weekends, and they wouldn't know where he was. Why were they waiting for him now?

He knew the difference, he admitted. For one thing, it was a weeknight. He usually came home after work on weeknights. He hadn't been home, and they knew he had the pickup. And, if pushed by their parents as to Jonas's whereabouts, Roseanne had probably told on him.

As he approached the driveway, he considered walking by. But that would only postpone the ordeal. No, he'd take this like a man. A 19-year-old man who's old enough to take care of himself and not answer to his parents for every move he makes, he thought to himself. Tilting his new hat low over his eyes, he strode in the back door, through the kitchen, and into the large family living room. The house was hot. His father, Fred, sat dozing in his olive-green recliner, clad only in his boxer shorts.

I could probably sneak upstairs and he'd never know it, Jonas realized. No, he told himself again. Face it like a man.

"Dad," he stated, "I'm home."

The 40-year-old Amish man jerked awake. His eyes—the same clear blue as his son's—focused on the tall young man standing in the doorway. They took in the stiff new blue jeans, western shirt, and big black hat. Jonas waited.

Chapter
3

"Nice hat," Fred said, rubbing his eyes. "Where do they sell hats like that in the middle of the night?"

As well as he knew his father, Jonas still got caught by surprise. Fred's sense of humor could come out at the most unexpected times. Jonas loved it, and enjoyed matching wits with his father.

"New store just opened up. Surprised you haven't heard about it—a 24-hour western store."

"In Wellsford? I can't believe I haven't seen it," Fred deadpanned.

"Actually, in Vicksburg."

"Must have been pretty special that you had to go there tonight."

"Yeah, they had Garth Brooks in the store doing a little concert."

"Uh huh. How'd you get there?"

"Drove Schmidt's pickup."

"Who went along?"

"Sue Ann Eash."

"Just Sue Ann?"

"Yep."

"You and Sue Ann went to Vicksburg in Schmidt's pickup to a Garth Brooks concert."

"That's right."

Fred was quiet for a long time. So long, in fact, that Jonas was ready to say good-night and go to bed. It was, after all, nearly 2:00 a.m.

"Well, I do appreciate you taking Sue Ann," Fred stated. "Now, take that hat off, and sit down, Jonas," he continued, and all lightheartedness was gone from his voice.

"You borrowed a truck so old it can't be trusted not to break down at any time. Who knows what works and what doesn't work on it. Suppose you got stopped. You could be in big trouble.

"Not to mention where you went," he continued, leaning forward toward Jonas in the rocker beside him. "Vicksburg, of all places! And you were there late at night!" his voice raised. "How can you forget what happened to Enos there? WHEN WILL YOU EVER LEARN?"

Fred ended with fire in his eyes, and then slumped back into his chair. After a moment, he stood up and began to walk out of the room. Stopping in the doorway, he stared at Jonas in the rocker, his head down, his eyes studying the braided rug on the floor.

"Sometimes I wonder if I'll still have a son named Jonas a year from now," Fred said, and left.

❖ ❖ ❖

Debbie didn't talk to Jonas that morning. Not when he arrived at 6:00 and she saw him step out of the pickup. Not when they passed each other while doing the chores. Not when he offered to help her feed the calves. Her silence drove Jonas crazy, because that wasn't Debbie. And he knew exactly why she was upset.

Finally, he couldn't stand it any longer. "Look, I'm sorry," he said, planting himself next to her as she placed a bucket of milk in front of a bawling calf. "I didn't know what to do. I took Sue Ann because she's such a big Garth Brooks fan."

"What are you doing tonight?" Debbie responded.

"I guess working in the field for Harlan," Jonas answered. "Why?"

"I'll bring you a snack. I'll ride with you on the tractor. We'll talk then."

❖ ❖ ❖

From his vantage point high in the cab of the huge 8830 John

Deere tractor, Jonas could see Debbie's car make its way down the country road and park in the ditch near the field. Shimmering waves of heat and dust hung in the air between them, and he was glad for the air-conditioned tractor cab. Approaching the end of the field, he swung the monster machine around with perfect timing, allowing the field cultivator behind it to till up to the edge of the sandy brown soil. He stopped the tractor and waited for Debbie to climb aboard.

"Brought you some fresh chocolate chip cookies," Debbie noted, closing the cab door behind her. She sat on the arm rest of the tractor seat as Jonas put the tractor in gear and pointed it back toward the hedge row of trees a distant half mile away.

"Thanks! You know I love your chocoate chip cookies," Jonas grinned, taking two.

"They're sort of a peace offering," Debbie volunteered.

"You didn't need to do that."

"I know I was a jerk this morning. But I was really disappointed."

"I know. I'm sorry."

"It's just that you get along so well with my folks, and I thought it'd be such a fun thing for the four of us to do together."

"It would have been. I'm sure I'd have had a great time."

"Then why? Why Sue Ann?"

"Like I said this morning, she's just such a big Garth fan. I wanted her to be able to see him."

"That's all?"

That's all? She wonders if that's all. Jonas's mind spun crazily. Just over two years ago, he would have taken Debbie automatically. They wouldn't be having this conversation. They'd be sitting in the tractor and she'd be teasing him about something. They'd have the Royals game on in the background. He'd go home and dream of Debbie....

He still liked her. But not in the same way. Ever since Enos's funeral, he'd decided to stick with Amish girls when it came to dating.

"Look Debbie, I took Sue Ann because she likes Garth. And because ... because she's Amish."

Jonas felt the tension between him and the girl seated so close in the tractor cab.

"So what, us worldly girls aren't good enough for you?" Debbie's voice was suddenly bitter and angry. "I don't party enough, right?"

"No, no, it's not that ..."

"What is it then? Huh?"

How could he explain it all. How could he explain the years of Amish upbringing. Years of being told people born Amish were meant to stay Amish. That if the children left the faith, God would hold the parents responsible.

How could he tell her the words of his parents: "If you marry outside the Amish, it will break our hearts." It wasn't that they didn't like her, or any of the other English young people in the community. They just wanted to keep their own in the fold.

"I know what it is," Debbie broke the silence. "You've decided you're going to stay Amish, haven't you? You're going to give up everything and go back. Right?"

"Probably. Sometime. I don't know when."

"Why not start now? You've got a girl already. You could start joining church together," the bitterness was back.

"I don't have a girl. And I'm not ready yet."

"You're not fooling me, Jonas. You're sweet on Sue Ann, and you're having fun driving her around in that old pickup. You want the best of both worlds. A sweet little Amish girl that you can do worldly things with. And then, when you've totally fallen in love, you'll go back to your horse and buggy, because it won't matter any more. You'll have her. You'll get married, have a dozen kids, and live happily ever after. Just like the church wants you to. Think about it, Jonas. Is that what you want?"

Jonas drove the tractor in shocked silence. Partly at Debbie's uncharacteristic sarcasm, and partly because what she said rang true. What could he say?

First, his dad got on his case for being in the world too much. Now Debbie was mad at the possibility that he'd stay Amish. All this because he'd taken Sue Ann to a concert.

Chapter 3

Sue Ann. He remembered. How could he forget? The song— what were the words again?

> *Our lives are better left to chance*
> *I could have missed the pain*
> *But I'd have had to miss the dance.*

Miss the dance—the evening with Sue Ann? No way—he'd take the pain.

Jonas glanced at Debbie. His blue eyes met hers, then they both looked away and rode in silence.

Chapter 4

Plans

A s far as Jonas was concerned, what he was about to do just didn't make sense. But he was going to do it anyway.

He left the Schmidt farm around 5:00 p.m. the Friday after the concert, driving the white pickup. He passed through Wellsford on his way home; arriving there, he parked the truck under the row of trees. Grabbing a can of horse grain and a lead rope, he walked out to the pasture where the family horses were grazing. He whistled for Lightning, but the big bay gelding ignored the summons. He doesn't want to pull that buggy on a hot August evening any more than I want to be in it, Jonas thought to himself. "C'mon, Lightning!" he called, shaking the can, "come get some grain!"

Lightning raised his head, pricked his ears forward, and studied Jonas. A stark white blaze ran the length of his face, starting above his large brown eyes and ending at his soft, velvet nose. It didn't take much to imagine it resembled a lightning bolt.

Jonas knew Lightning would give in and come up for the grain. In the spring, when the pasture fescue grass grew long and lush, tempting a horse with grain was more of a challenge. His stomach was full and taste buds satisfied. But a summer's worth of grazing, plus the hot Kansas sun and wind, had taken its toll on the grass. Now the grain looked mighty good.

"How're you doing, big boy?" Jonas said, reaching for Lightning's halter as he drew close. He snapped the lead rope to

the halter, and poured the grain into his hand. Lightning folded his big soft lips around the corn and oats mixture, then nuzzled the can for more. "That's all, let's go," Jonas said, leading Lightning away from the rest of the horses and back to the barn.

Jonas quickly hitched Lightning up to his single-seat open buggy. He'd been hitching horses to buggies and farm equipment since he was five or six years old. Lightning stomped and swatted at the pesky flies, so Jonas sprayed him thoroughly with a fly repellent. Leaving the horse tied at the hitching post, Jonas ran into the house, took the stairs to his room two at a time, and quickly changed into his blue jeans and western shirt. He noticed the cowboy hat hanging on a hook on the wall. Why not, he thought, and set the hat on his head so it rode low over his eyes.

Chapter
4

"Where do you think you're going, all doozied up?" Roseanne's challenge caught Jonas before he could slip out the back door.

"Wellsford. Ball game," he responded. "Anything to eat around here?"

"There will be, at supper time," his mother Esther answered, coming into the kitchen with a bucketful of fresh-from-the-garden cucumbers, corn, tomatoes, and zucchini. "Why don't you stay around once and eat with us?"

"Don't have time," Jonas responded, grabbing some cookies from the strawberry-shaped cookie jar. "See you later!"

❖ ❖ ❖

Forty minutes later, Jonas tied Lightning to the hitching post near the Wellsford ball diamond. I could have been here a long time ago, Jonas thought, but no! Rather than just coming here in the pickup right after work, I had to go home, catch the horse and hitch him up, then drive the horse and buggy here. It doesn't make sense, but I did it.

Why? Was he trying to please his parents to make up for the trip into Vicksburg? Was he afraid of showing up late at home again with the truck? He wasn't sure. It just seemed like the thing to do.

Jonas looked around to see who else was at the game. A number of other Amish guys were hanging around, waiting for the current game to end and theirs to begin. They were clustered around a young man and a van, neither of which Jonas recognized. He strolled over toward the group, noticing the van sported an Illinois tag.

"... stopped by to see what's happening here and if anybody wants to run to Missouri tomorrow," the stranger was saying.

"What's happening in Missouri?" Jonas asked the newcomer, who appeared to be in his mid-to-late 20's.

"Barn party," Mervin Smucker answered. "I came down from Illinois yesterday, and stopped by Johnstown. They said they're havin' a dance and party tomorrow night. Figured I'd see if anybody here wants to go."

Jonas glanced around at the group of guys. They could fill the van in a hurry.

"Sounds good to me," Jonas answered. "Anybody else?"

None of the guys had anything better to do the next day than make a four-hour trip to Missouri for an Amish barn party.

❖ ❖ ❖

Although a number of Amish girls showed up at the game to watch the guys play, Sue Ann wasn't one of them. She probably had to work, Jonas reasoned. He'd stop by the restaurant after the game to talk to her. He was curious about how her parents reacted to their trip into Vicksburg.

Just after 11:00 p.m., Jonas turned Lightning into the parking lot of The Deutschland Restaurant. Good, her bike is still here, he noted. She must be closing up. He sipped on the huge cherry limeade he'd picked up at the local hamburger joint. In most other towns, having a horse and buggy pull up at a fast-food drive-thru would throw the person at the window for a loop. The people in

Wellsford were used to it. The young woman at the window this time, though, had seemed to notice something else, Jonas recalled. "Nice hat," she said. "Nicer than those straw things I usually see you guys wearing." The compliment embarrassed and flattered Jonas who'd flashed her a quick smile before slapping Lightning's reins and moving him out of the drive-thru lane.

Now, waiting for Sue Ann, he noticed how hot the hat was. Lifting the hat and wiping the perspiration from his forehead, he resolved to wait for cooler weather to wear it again.

"Hey, what are you doing here?" Sue Ann approached the buggy, her voice reflecting pleasant surprise.

"Thought I'd stop by and see if you survived your parents last night," Jonas answered. "Let's tie your bike on here and I'll take you home."

Sue Ann lived less than a mile out of town, and it wouldn't take Lightning long to get there. It was barely after 11:00 p.m.— way too early to go home. They could go to Sam's apartment—he knew a lot of the kids had gone there after the game. But he really wanted to talk to Sue Ann, and Sam's was no place to do that. They'd just take the long way to Sue Ann's, he planned, flipping on the switch of the battery-powered buggy lights.

Sue Ann didn't question Jonas when he didn't turn Lightning down her road. She too had no desire to go home when the night was so young.

"My dad was waiting up for me," Jonas said. "How about yours?"

"They weren't waiting up, but I had to tell them in the morning. Dad's hardly talking to me, and Mom—she's talking too much."

Jonas chuckled. "She's letting you have it, huh? What's she saying?"

"She was worried because she didn't know where I was. She was worried that something had happened to me. And of course she was worried about me not being a member of the church if something bad really did happen."

"Sounds familiar. My dad was mad that we went to Vicksburg in an ol' beater pickup that belonged to somebody else, and that we were there at night. He reminded me about Enos."

"Mom mentioned that too. She's not happy about me going out with another guy with a vehicle. They didn't like it at all when I dated Sam, and they were so relieved when we broke up. Last night, Mom said, 'Why can't you date somebody in a horse and buggy? Somebody like Orville or Nathan?'" Sue Ann's voice sounded just like her mom's, and Jonas chuckled.

"You're in a horse and buggy tonight," he noted. "What could be more wholesome than this?" His voice took on a dramatic flair. "Here we are, under the vast expanse of the Kansas sky, with nothing but the stars to entertain us! Aren't we being good tonight?"

Sue Ann giggled before answering, "Yeah, but I don't think they trust you. They think you're being influenced too much by the Schmidts."

"In what ways?"

"Well, the pickup, of course. And they've heard rumors that the Schmidts are doing their best to get you and Debbie together."

"And tell me again how that's any of their concern?"

"If I'm out with you, Mom thinks it is. Plus, she's worried about what people will think when they find out we went to Vicksburg to the concert. She just knows people are saying 'Those Eashs have no control over their daughter.' And then she talks about what a bad influence I am on my younger sisters."

"I didn't realize I was out with such a *bad girl*," Jonas chuckled again.

"You know what else she said?" Sue Ann smiled in the dark. "She said she hopes that when I'm her age, I'll have a daughter just like me, and then I can see what she went through."

"I'm sure you will," Jonas grinned to himself.

❖ ❖ ❖

Neither Jonas nor Sue Ann wanted to say good-bye that night. Their comfortable talking had turned to a cozy silence as they held hands during the last mile to her home. Jonas turned Lightning into the Eash farmstead and stopped him under a big cottonwood tree in the middle of the yard. He switched off the buggy lights, and in the pitch darkness, the young couple kissed away the moments.

Chapter
4

Finally, when Lightning got impatient and threatened to walk off, Jonas said he should be going. He grabbed a flashlight from under the seat, jumped off the buggy, and led Lightning to the hitching post. After tying him up, he unloaded Sue Ann's bike, and then the pair found their way in the blackness to the house.

"Follow me," Sue Ann whispered, taking Jonas's hand. She knew her way around the house without a light, and tiptoed to the stairs leading up to her room.

Trusting her hand, Jonas followed Sue Ann. He couldn't help but remember Debbie's reaction, years ago, when she found out some of the Amish dating customs. Like couples spending time together in the girl's bedroom.

"My parents would never allow that!" Debbie had exclaimed.

"Do they let you ride with a guy at night in his car?" Jonas had replied.

"Well sure."

"And do they know what you're doing, and where you might be parking in that car?"

"No."

"I'll bet nothing more happens among Amish couples in their rooms than what other people do in their cars," Jonas had declared.

Debbie hadn't believed him, but he knew it to be true. At 19, he'd done his share of dating. Spending time with his date in her room was normal. In fact, often there was more than one couple in the room. And contrary to what Debbie and seemingly the rest of the world assumed, they weren't being any more intimate than other teenagers sitting on couches, watching videos.

"That's the last step," Sue Ann's whisper brought Jonas back to the present. "My room's just around the corner here. Do you want to come in?"

Did he want to go in? Was there any question? But ...

"I'd love to," Jonas whispered back. "But I'm afraid I'd never get away, and it's Friday night. Tomorrow's my day off, so Dad'll expect me up early to help him. And I have to put in some good hours in the morning, because I'm leaving in the afternoon for Missouri."

"That's okay. Maybe another time," Sue Ann said lightly. "I'll see you when you get back from Missouri."

"And I'll try to remember that it's better to pick you up in a horse and buggy than in a pickup," Jonas smiled in the blackness. "Do me a favor. Tell your mom I brought you home in a buggy."

"Knowing her, she probably knows that already."

❖ ❖ ❖

As far as the rest of his family was concerned, they'd already let Jonas sleep in when Fred sent Roseanne to wake Jonas at 6:00 a.m. But it seemed much too early to him.

"Get up, you lazy bum," Jonas heard groggily. "Dad says you should be helping with the chores. He has a lot for you to do today."

Jonas rolled over and groaned. His weekend off from the Schmidts, and his dad had the day planned for him. Then he remembered ... Missouri! He'd better get a lot done this morning.

"You gonna stay home weekends now?" Thirteen-year-old Orie nudged Jonas at the breakfast table. "Seein's how you're always gone during the weeknights lately, we're wondering if you're gonna be home weekends."

"Yeah, we thought you could help us break that colt," David, 14, chimed in.

"Jonas is going to help me fix the hay wagon today," Fred stated, reaching for the plate of bacon and fried eggs. "Crazy team ran off with it the other day when I was going to get a load of alfalfa," he said, addressing Jonas. "Rabbit jumped in front of them. They didn't stop 'til they got home."

"Did the wagon stay with them?" Jonas hadn't been around the house enough to hear this most recent episode. That team of three-year-old horses, Molly and Mae, was young and still quite spooky. Runaway stories were all too common with them.

"Yeah, but *I* didn't," Fred admitted, and the kids around the table burst into laughter.

"He says he bailed out, but we think he just plumb *fell off!*" David guffawed.

"That wagon was all over the road and I had no place to brace myself," Fred tried to defend himself. "You think it's so funny— I'll turn that team over to you, young man."

"You should have seen Mae and Molly come tearing in here!" ten-year-old Robert pitched in. "And that big hay wagon bouncing behind them, already missing a wheel!" he laughed.

"So, we have some repairs to do," Fred concluded.

"I'm just glad it wasn't me that wrecked that wagon," Jonas noted. "I'd have never heard the end of it."

"You should've seen it, Jonas!" Robert's twin, Rebecca, repeated. "And you should have seen Dad come limping home."

"Eat your breakfast, Rebecca," Fred said.

Chapter 5

ℬarn 𝒫arty

Mervin Smucker's 1978, slightly-worse-for-the-wear Ford van rumbled into the Bontrager yard shortly after lunch that August Saturday. Jonas had warned his father he'd need to quit working when Mervin showed up, and he'd half-expected his dad to complain about his never being around to help. Instead, Fred had told Jonas he was glad he was going to Missouri with a group of Amish guys, rather than hanging around with English girls. Although he didn't come out and say it, Jonas knew his father meant Debbie. What he *had* said made his personal preference quite obvious: "Too bad you guys aren't taking girls along from here. Like Sue Ann. She's going to make somebody a nice wife."

"Yeah right, Dad," Jonas agreed, and loped to the van waiting for him.

Sixteen guys occupied the seats and floor of the 12-passenger vehicle when they opened the door for Jonas to get in. Noting that his seating options were an armrest, the floor between the driver's and front passenger's seats, or another guy's lap, Jonas opted for the floor. Maybe he could grab a better seat when they all got out for a pit stop.

Mervin, Jonas found out, was a Conservative Mennonite from Iowa. His parents had grown up Amish but left the church and joined the Mennonites when they got married. Single and 28, Mervin was a popular "taxi" for the Amish young folks in his community as well as in other states. He kept busy nearly every weekend, and often during the week as well, hauling Amish kids. He made decent money at it, and he had a great time at the parties. With his many trips back and forth between Amish communities, he was also a carrier of the latest news and gossip.

"So, what's new in Iowa?" Jonas queried. "Anything exciting happening?"

"Well, you've probably heard about the ruckus going on around tractors."

"Bits and pieces. Some people trying to switch?"

"Yeah. There's talk. It isn't close to a church vote yet, but I bet it comes to that."

"You think it'd pass?"

"No way. They'll never get 100 percent of the people to vote yes."

"Back in Gainesboro, you know, they got 100 percent a couple of years ago to go from steel wheels to air tires on their tractors."

"Yeah, but they already had the tractors. Moving from horses to tractors is a bigger deal. It won't happen. The bishop in that Iowa church is too strong. And he has a lot of sons and daughters with families. They'll all vote against it."

"I wonder if it'll ever come up in Wellsford," Jonas said thoughtfully.

"It's bound to. Someday."

"I know what my Dad would do. He's dead set against modernizing."

"Really? Why?" Merv wondered.

"Because he thinks one thing leads to another. I've heard him say it a million times. 'One year it's tractors. Then air tires. Next they'll be putting cabs on the tractors and taking the family to town in them.'"

"And next thing you know, the only time they'll use their buggies is to go to church, and the rest of the time they'll ride around in their tractors," Merv continued.

"Why, before long, in a hundred years or so, they'll drop the buggies completely and buy cars!" Jonas feigned disgust and disbelief.

Merv laughed, then turned serious. "Nope, that'll never happen."

"I know. People might leave so they can have more modern things, but the Amish tradition is too strong. It hasn't changed much over the years, and it won't."

"You going to stay Amish?" Merv turned to look down at Jonas on the floor.

Jonas didn't look up. "Don't know," he muttered, then added, "Probably."

"Find yourself a nice little Amish girl, settle down, make lots of babies! It's not such a bad life!" Merv teased.

"You should talk!"

"Hey, the Amish wouldn't have me!"

"I mean the settling down and having babies part. Don't tell me you can't find a Mennonite girl who's dying to ride around in this *cool* van with you!"

Merv laughed, then answered, "That's the problem. I'm too busy hauling Amish kids around in this van to have a dating life. Besides, where would I put her?" he motioned toward the packed interior.

"You've got a point," Jonas conceded. "So, tell me about this party."

"It's supposed to be a big one. Some Amish guys from Indiana have a band, and they're going to be there. They've got a great reputation, so that'll pull the kids in. I imagine there'll be a couple hundred."

"I've heard about that band," Jonas answered.

"For guys who just started playing a few years ago, they're awesome."

"Can't wait to hear 'em."

❖ ❖ ❖

The van arrived in the Johnstown community several hours

before the barn party would begin, and the guys knew exactly what to do with that time. The Miller brothers were the first to give instructions to Mervin, directing him to drop them off at the home of their cousins. Several others had specific girls they wanted to pick up.

"Hey, Jonas, this is Barbara," Joe Hostetler introduced the girl who'd just climbed in the van and found his lap to be the only place left to sit. "I bet she has a sister or cousin or *somebody* for you this weekend! Don't you, Barbara?"

Barbara, a fair-skinned, blond, green-eyed beauty smiled down at Jonas, who never had found a seat better than the floor. "I do, as a matter of fact. She'll be at the party. I'll get you together there."

"Hey, I'd like to get together with *them*!" Edwin Keim yelled from his position scrunched against one of the windows. The van had just passed an open buggy packed with Amish girls. "Stop the van! Let me into that buggy!"

Laughing, Mervin slammed on the brakes, throwing everyone in the van forward. Edwin climbed over several bodies on his way to the door, then slid it open and half-fell out. He stuck his thumb in the air as the buggy approached.

"Van's too full," he deadpanned to the three young women in the buggy. "You got any room for a man from Kansas who needs to get to a party in Missouri?"

Giggling, the girls looked at each other, at Edwin, and at the van full of faces watching them.

"I suppose there's always room for one more," the girl holding the reins volunteered. "If you can find a place to sit."

"EEE YOW!" Edwin whooped. "I'll just stand back there behind the seat. Hey, Abe!" he yelled toward the van. "You wanna come back here with me? The view's great, if you know what I mean!"

Abe didn't need a second invitation, and moments later the van continued down the winding road with two fewer guys, while a buggy load of three had increased to five.

After a number of planned and unplanned stops at homes and along the country roads, Mervin's vanload found its way into Johnstown to the local hamburger joint. About half of the original guys were in the van, and just about that many new girls had replaced them. Jonas couldn't help but wonder what awaited him at the party. This sister/cousin/whatever of Barbara's—if she was pretty and fun, why didn't she have a date already? Why? Because she's probably 300 pounds and pushing 30, Jonas shuddered.

Around dusk, the van made its way out of Johnstown and through the gentle hills of the community. Mervin knew from experience that he'd have to keep a sharp eye out for buggies, especially with the hills and curves hiding them until almost the last minute. Although quite visible with reflector tape and lights, the buggies were deceiving because their speed was so much slower than other vehicles. Anyone coming up on one from behind and thinking it was a vehicle moving at the expected speed could be in for a bad, potentially tragic, surprise. Mervin ignored the teenage craziness going on in his van and concentrated on the road in front of him.

"Lotsa buggies going to the party," Jonas observed from the floor beside Mervin's seat.

"You know it. And cars too. I told you it'll be a big one."

"How far out here is it?"

"Not too far. Just seems like it, with these hills slowing us down. Fact is, I think it's just around this curve."

As they rounded the curve, Jonas could see the outline of a farm in the settling darkness. The van lights brought the road ahead alive with the reflective tape of a long row of buggies. Cars, pickups, and vans—many of them with tags from Illinois, Michigan, Indiana, and Oklahoma—intermingled with the horse-drawn buggies.

"Where's the family?" Jonas wondered out loud.

"I heard they're on vacation in Colorado," Mervin explained.

"The parents took the younger kids and left the older ones home to do the chores."

"Looks like they'll have more than some cows to clean up after—after tonight," Jonas remarked.

"Hey, I'm sure it was their idea," Mervin noted. "They've got the perfect place for a party."

No kidding, Jonas thought, as they drew closer to the large white two-story barn. Nestled into the hillside, the barn's wide doors to its hay storage area stood open, and a nice-looking van with a trailer was pulled up to the doors.

"The band's here," Mervin noted. "They've got a generator in that trailer. Powers their equipment."

Jonas smiled at the contrast between the Coleman lanterns lighting the barn and the generator-powered electrical instruments. "They got strobe lights too?" he chuckled.

"Who knows?" Mervin said. "Guess we'll find out."

❖ ❖ ❖

"Jonas!"

Jonas turned to see Barbara, the pretty blond they'd picked up for Joe earlier that evening. Barbara … and another girl about her age.

"This is Naomi," Barbara introduced. "She's my cousin, and she'd be happy to be your date tonight."

"Nice to meet you," Jonas grinned, and if Naomi could have seen his blue eyes in the dark, she'd have known how relieved, and pleased, he was. His eyes took in her light green Amish dress, her long mahogany hair, the freckles on her red-brown tanned face, and her bare brown feet. Pretty, in a wholesome, healthy kind of way, he thought. She's wearing a dress, but her hair is down. She must be in the process of joining church—taking catechism, slowly getting into the accepted clothes and lifestyle, he mused.

"You guys came up from Wellsford?" Naomi asked in a soft, pleasant voice as they strolled toward the big barn.

"Yep. We heard this was the place to be this weekend, so we piled into a van, and here we are."

"I have relatives in Wellsford. My mom's sister and her husband and family—Rachel and Cris Eash."

Rachel and Cris Eash, Sue Ann's parents. How about that, Jonas smiled.

"So Sue Ann is your cousin?" he remarked.

"Yes! Why didn't she come along?"

"I think she had to work," Jonas tried to sound nonchalant. "Plus it was just a bunch of us guys coming. Man, is this a party or what," he changed the subject as they approached the barn. Rock n' roll music poured out of the large barn doors, and the farmyard was crowded with vehicles, horses, buggies, and small cliques of young people. While a good number of them listened and danced in the barn, other guys and gals gathered around pickup tailgates, sipping drinks out of coolers, laughing and talking.

"Let's get a drink before we go in," Jonas suggested. "What do you want?"

"Anything diet," Naomi answered. "Coke if they have it."

Jonas fished a Diet Coke out of one cooler for Naomi, then moved to another cooler for a Bud Lite. Cans in hand, they joined the dozens of youth lined along the barn's walls, soaking up the energy of the band and the music in the light of Coleman lanterns.

The evening passed quickly. Jonas enjoyed dancing and visiting with Naomi—she really was a nice girl. Maybe it was just his imagination, but he could see similarities between her and Sue Ann. Midnight came and went. The band took a break, and Edwin Keim had an idea.

"See that big rope up there?" Edwin nudged Jonas as they sat leaning against the barn wall.

Jonas could barely see the rope in the dimly lit interior, but he knew it was there. Most barns had them in their haylofts—they were used to pull the sling full of loose hay up from the ground and into the barn.

"I'm thinking a guy could climb up the wall, grab that rope, and have one heck of a swing," Edwin slurred. Jonas knew Edwin's trips to the cooler had muddled his thinking a bit, but what he said made sense. Yes, a guy could swing on that rope.

"I'm thinking I need to do that," Edwin stated, and stood up. Apparently Edwin wasn't the first one with the idea, because in days long gone by, someone had nailed a makeshift ladder to the side of the wall—the top of it just within a long arm's reach of the heavy hemp rope. Spotting the ladder, Edwin let out a whoop and quickly climbed it. Reaching for the rope, he held on, wrapped one leg around it, and pushed off with the other.

Chapter
5

"Look out below!" he hollered, and swung out over the floor, barely missing some unsuspecting couples who hadn't been paying attention to his shenanigans.

Edwin had started something. And soon the guys, lining up to take their turns, began imagining something more—something more adventurous and dangerous. "Let's open the big door on top and swing outside," one of them said.

"That's a 30-foot drop to the ground," another one warned.

"So who's dropping?" the daredevil asked.

So it was that at 1:30 a.m., a dozen of the guys were taking turns swinging on the rope, out into the black Missouri night, and back into the barn. A group watched from the barn floor, cheering and jeering them on. If anyone noticed the rope's creaking and groaning during each swing, they didn't think much of it. And in the darkness, no one could see the condition of the old rope.

"Hey, Jonas, I haven't seen you do it yet!" Edwin stopped by where Jonas and Naomi sat, watching. "C'mon! Show us your stuff!"

"Naw, I'll pass," Jonas answered.

"Chicken! What's she gonna think of you?" Edwin nodded at Naomi. "Don't be such a wuss!"

Against his better judgment, and certainly his desires, Jonas gave in. He rubbed his hands on the floor for some traction, then climbed the rickety ladder. Reaching for the rope, he took a deep breath and pushed off.

Within seconds he found himself suspended in midair outside the barn, and just as quickly the rope swing brought him in again. Another trip out. Don't think about falling, he told himself. Just hang on and ride it out.

One more trip out, back in, and the momentum was gone. Jonas dropped to the floor, then stood up and walked casually back to his place. "If you're so brave, Edwin, why don't you do it with just one hand?" he challenged.

Edwin stared at Jonas, and a slow smile spread across his face. "I just might take you up on that."

When Edwin's turn came for the rope, he stood at the top of the ladder. "This one's for you, Jonas!" he yelled.

With that, he swung out, one arm wrapped around the rope, the other waving crazily. In a flash he disappeared into the blackness, and at that moment, the frazzled old rope high above them shredded.

They heard Edwin scream.

Chapter 6

Family

Jonas and the others who'd been watching Edwin swinging on the rope ran out the big barn doors, around the corner, and down the steep hillside. They couldn't see very well where they were going, but they knew Edwin was somewhere below them. Naomi stopped to grab a lantern and followed them down the hill, her bare feet flying through the dry grass.

"Edwin! Are you okay?" Jonas knelt beside Edwin, who lay at the bottom of the incline, clutching his ankle.

"I'm fine," Edwin said through clenched teeth. "'Cept for my ankle. Hurts like—"

"Where's Merv?" Jonas asked the group gathered around them. "Find him. He'll have to take Edwin to the emergency room."

"I'll be okay," Edwin said, trying to stand up. "Don't need no emergency room. Just park me next to one of those coolers. I'll be feeling no pain."

"You're going," Jonas stated. "If it's broken, it's got to be set."

So, amidst much protest, Edwin allowed himself to be helped to Merv's van. Merv said he'd take care of it from there—no need for anyone else to go along.

A damper had been thrown on the party, and, it being 2:30 a.m., a number of the youth decided it was time to head out. Naomi told Jonas they'd be going to her place with her brother and his girlfriend. The two couples got into an open single-seat buggy and left the farmyard. "It's not too far," Naomi said from her position on Jonas's lap. "Just around the curve and down the road a bit."

The ride with a girl he'd met several hours ago and two youth he didn't know at all made Jonas smile to himself in the warm humid Missouri night. Debbie would never understand this, he smiled. Not that he cared. Sue Ann, she'd understand. Sue Ann. Who was she out with tonight?

"You can go to church with us in the morning, Jonas," Naomi's voice broke into his thoughts.

"Thanks. Uh ... we'll see," Jonas evaded.

"I hear you," Naomi's brother chuckled. "I wouldn't go either if I didn't have to. She has to go because she's taking catechism. Actually, we are too," his arms wrapped tighter around the waist of the girl on his lap.

"Bet your parents are thrilled to have you both joining at the same time," Jonas commented.

"It's a big relief for them, sure," Naomi said. "What about Sue Ann? She's older than we are and she still hasn't joined. I know my mom and Aunt Rachel have written about that in their letters."

"Who knows," Jonas was noncommittal. He wondered what else the letters said. Did they talk about a trip to Vicksburg to a Garth Brooks concert?

The horse and buggy crossed a bridge and shortly after turned into a dark farmyard set just off the road, surrounded by trees. Jonas and Naomi jumped off the buggy and walked toward the house. The other two stayed behind to unhitch the horse and lead him to the corral.

❖ ❖ ❖

Four short hours later, Jonas found himself kneeling for prayer at the breakfast table with Naomi's family. Most of the family had been up for several hours already doing the morning chores. Even Naomi's brother. He probably hadn't slept at all, Jonas figured. That's what being in love does to a person, Jonas thought. He'll be nodding off in church for sure.

"So you're from Wellsford?" Naomi's father addressed Jonas, passing him a plate of fried mush. "Who are your parents?"

"Fred and Esther Bontrager."

"Ah yes, I know them. And you probably know Rachel and Cris Eash—Rachel and my wife are sisters."

"Yes," Jonas answered, adding a fried egg to his plate.

"Their daughter Sue Ann. Is she still running with the young folks?"

"Yeah, she is. I guess some people wonder why she hasn't joined church yet," Jonas volunteered.

Naomi's parents cast knowing glances at each other before her father responded.

"They probably do. Yes, they probably do. We're so thankful that Naomi and Mark are going to be joining soon," he paused. "You'll be going to church with us this morning?"

Jonas concentrated on choosing the best slice of fresh tomato from the plate in front of him before answering.

"I think we'll be heading back to Kansas," he said, not knowing at all what time the van would show up. "I'll need to wait here for them."

"We'd sure enjoy having you go with us and staying around for the afternoon," Naomi's father said, then winked at her. "Wouldn't we, Naomi?"

"Of course," she agreed, and Jonas knew the reddish-brown color of her face wasn't just from the sun. It was still too early to get much light through the kitchen windows, but he could see enough to confirm his impressions of the night before—Naomi was cute. Her green eyes looked a bit tired this morning, but they were still smiling.

"I wish I could," Jonas half-lied. He didn't want to go to church, but spending time with Naomi would be all right. But he couldn't.

"I really do have to wait for the van."

❖ ❖ ❖

Jonas fell asleep on the living room couch and woke with a start to the sound of a horn honking outside the house. For a second he didn't know where he was—the room wasn't familiar! Then he remembered—Naomi's family. They weren't back from church—what time was it?

The clock said 2:00 p.m. Church was out and everyone would have eaten the meal of sandwiches, fresh vegetables, and pie. After cleanup and visiting, they'd be heading home. There'd be a lot of buggies on the road. He ran out to the van.

Sliding the door open, he groaned. His seating options weren't much better than when he got in the van 24 hours ago. The only "improvement" was that a cooler now sat in the space between Merv's seat and the passenger seat where Edwin sat. Fine, he'd sit on the cooler, Jonas thought. Merv would probably need somebody to help keep him awake anyway.

"Careful," Edwin mumbled, half-asleep. "Don't even get close to my ankle."

Jonas noticed a light cast on Edwin's ankle. "Is it broken?" he asked.

"Yep," Merv answered. "We were at the hospital most of the night. Got back at 8:00 this morning, slept in the van, got a bite to eat, and started picking up guys. By the way, do you remember where we dropped the Miller boys off yesterday?"

Jonas hadn't noticed that everyone wasn't in the van—it looked full to him. Apparently they were still missing two guys.

"Not really. I wasn't paying much attention."

"I guess I wasn't either. I just drove where they told me to go. Out here with these curves and hills, it's hard to keep track. Not like in Iowa or Kansas, where everything is marked off in miles."

"So we don't have everyone and we don't know where to find them," Jonas concluded.

"Something like that," Merv half-laughed.

"Have you asked the rest of the guys?"

"Yeah. Nobody knows. They all said you would."

Jonas didn't have a clue.

"We could leave them," he joked. "Maybe they'll hitchhike back to Wellsford."

"I've considered that," Merv agreed.

"Or we can spend the whole day driving from house to house."

"I haven't considered that."

"Okay, then let's go back to where the party was and see if anybody's there who knows," Jonas suggested.

They did. One of the young folks thought he remembered some local Miller kids who'd said something about their cousins being there. He gave them directions to the Miller farm. Arriving at the farm, they saw that the family had just returned from church. "You talk to them," Merv said to Jonas.

"Why me?" Jonas complained, but he slid open the door and stepped out. "We're looking for the Miller brothers from Wellsford," he answered the questions in the Amish man's eyes. "They wouldn't happen to be here, would they?"

"Something that might have been two boys stumbled into the house and up the stairs during the night," the man in the black hat, pants, and vest said, stroking his long black beard. "'Course I haven't seen or heard anything since, so it might have all been a bad dream," he added. "You're welcome to look."

Jonas went into the house, found the stairway and ran up the steps. Loud snoring led him to the right bedroom, and he emerged from the house moments later with the Miller boys in tow.

"Oh, them!" The man was standing by the van, talking to Merv. "My brother's boys. It's been nice having you here for a visit—tell the family hi!" his eyes twinkled under the somber black hat. He winked at Merv. "I remember when their dad and I were teenagers and we spent weekends with our cousins like this. Drove our parents crazy. Now we're the parents," he shook his head. "Come again, boys!" he chuckled at his nephews. "Drive carefully," he told Merv, patting the van.

❖ ❖ ❖

46

Chapter 6

As Mervin's van approached the Bontrager farm early that evening, Jonas noticed the yard was full of buggies. What in the ... Was someone having a birthday? August. Who had a birthday in August? His mother! Today was his mother's birthday!

"Party at your house, Jonas?" Merv asked, turning into the driveway.

"My mom's birthday!" Jonas answered. "I forgot all about it until I saw the buggies."

The van stopped. Jonas had no more than stepped out before he was surrounded by siblings and cousins—children who were barely walking all the way up to his brothers, David and Orie. Every single one was barefoot, and everyone was smiling. The younger children idolized Jonas; the others just thought it was cool to have a 19-year-old around for the evening. Jonas's 10-year-old sister, Rebecca, grabbed his hand and said, "Mommy didn't think you'd be here for her birthday, but I told her you would."

"And how did you know that?" Jonas addressed his youngest sister, but his eyes were on the smallest cousin in the bunch. Barely over a year, the little girl reached out to him and drooled a grin. Jonas crouched down and scooped the baby in his arms. "And how's my favorite little Letha?"

Letha rode happily in Jonas's arms as they walked toward the house, Rebecca prattling nonstop about how she knew Jonas would be home. "So I was right," she concluded, then ran to tell her mother the story all over again.

Esther's eyes lit up when her son walked into the kitchen. She really hadn't expected him at all—he wasn't ever home on Sunday evenings. Maybe he was finally growing up into a man— a man who thought about people other than himself. A man who knew how much certain things could mean to a woman, whether

that be his mother or his wife. Jonas had made a point of being here for her 40th birthday, and that meant the world to her.

"I'm happy you could make it," she said simply, and smiled at Jonas. "We're almost ready to eat."

"Happy Birthday," he replied. "I didn't bring any black balloons. Sorry about that."

Esther put her hand on her tall son's strong shoulder and said, "That's okay. I'm just glad you're here."

Jonas went back outside and joined the men sitting at the picnic table and on benches nearby. Several of them acknowledged his arrival, including his father, Fred, but they seemed to be in a heavy discussion.

"... getting to the point where a person can't farm enough with horses to make a living," one of Jonas's uncles was saying. "We need tractors to be able to work more acres."

"Bigger isn't better," Fred stated emphatically. "It's just giving in to what everybody around us is doing. Always trying to get more land. More land, more debts. They're never satisfied, and they're never any better off."

"You really think Jonas will be able to make a living with horses?" the uncle countered. "Come on, Fred, being realistic isn't the same as giving in to the world."

"And I hope, when the time comes, Jonas will respect our way of life enough to stay *with horses* and still make a good life for his wife and family," Fred looked directly into his son's eyes.

So, the tractor issue had come to Wellsford, Jonas realized. And to his family. Despite the warm Kansas wind on his back, a shiver went down Jonas's spine.

Tractors

A frigid arctic blast invaded Kansas late in October, bringing with it an early snowfall. Jonas shuddered in the old white pickup rumbling its way to the Schmidt dairy early one Monday morning. Be glad there's a little bit of heat coming out of the heater, he reminded himself. If you were in a buggy, you wouldn't have even that.

Not to mention the insulated coveralls he was wearing, he thought. They had to be warmer than what his father would don before he went out to do the morning chores. Fred would just increase the layers of homemade shirts, jackets, and pants to build in as much warmth as possible. The cozy convenience of insulated coveralls wasn't an option for Amish church members.

Jonas didn't know why. It was just one of those things. In fact, in some communities in other states, men weren't allowed to wear stocking caps or hoods over their heads in the bitter winter cold. I'll never move there, Jonas resolved. I hate the cold.

Florida. That's where he should be right now. Sue Ann was down there, along with half a dozen other Wellsford young folks. He should have gone too.

He'd heard about Sue Ann's plans a few days after his week-end in Missouri in August. He'd stopped by the restaurant at closing time to say hi and tell Sue Ann he'd met her cousin Naomi. That's when she'd told him she'd heard over the weekend about a group of kids going to Florida to work for the winter. Many

Amish from around the United States, most of them retired, liked to "winter" in Sunset, Florida. Young people could easily find jobs there in restaurants, construction, and other support services.

"I might as well go now while I can," Sue Ann had said. "I don't have anything else keeping me here this winter. Besides, I can lay out and tan all winter." Sue Ann's dark eyes sparkled. "Why don't you come too?"

Jonas had considered it. For one thing, he'd had to admit to himself he was disappointed that Sue Ann thought she didn't have any reason to stay in Wellsford. It wasn't like they were going steady or anything. Yet he'd been hoping their relationship would grow, and he thought she felt the same way. He could go to Florida and see what happened....

But when it came right down to it, Jonas wasn't ready to leave his job. The Schmidts depended on him a lot to help with the chores. If he left, they'd have to hire someone else. Harlan had been so good to him—Jonas just couldn't see himself saying, "I'm leaving for the winter. I'd like my job back this spring." And what about his heifers—the ones Harlan had given him. How could he expect Harlan to care for them through the cold Kansas winter while he soaked up the sun in Florida? No, he couldn't go.

So here he was, beginning another week of work. Jonas turned the stubborn steering wheel of the '67 Ford, and it slowly responded, rounding the corner onto the Schmidt farmyard. The truck was getting harder to turn all the time, and this frigid weather didn't help. Jonas pulled his stocking cap low over his forehead and neck and stepped out into the biting north wind.

❖ ❖ ❖

"So what's this I hear about some of the Amish wanting to get tractors?" Harlan asked Jonas as he stuck a casserole in the microwave at lunch that day. The men were on their own—Lynne was working part time at the school. She'd left some food already prepared, and instructions for the rest. "Make a fruit salad," her note said. Jonas was working on that part, slicing apples and bananas into a bowl that already held large, lush green grapes.

"I guess it's true," Jonas answered Harlan's question. "They're saying they can't farm as much as they need to with horses."

"Actually, I'm surprised they've held out this long," Harlan noted, opening a bag of homemade bread and putting several slices on a plate.

Chapter 7

"Why?"

"It's just not realistic. Surely you can see the difference. You drive big equipment here and then you go home and work with horses. Do you really think Amish farmers can continue to make a living with horses?"

"My dad says bigger isn't always better," Jonas repeated, and then the irony of his words hit him. It hadn't been very long ago that, in discussions with his father, he'd presented Harlan's—the world's—side of the issue. Now he was defending his dad!

"I'd expect him to say that," Harlan replied, glancing at Jonas as he opened the microwave door. "He's stuck in a religious tradition that won't allow him to grow. But I'm kinda surprised at you. Are you buying into that belief too?"

"I'm not buying into anything. I'm just saying that maybe there are two sides to this issue."

"No doubt there are." Harlan set the casserole down on the table. "Bring your salad, and let's talk about them."

Jonas and Harlan bowed their heads for a brief silent prayer, then helped themselves to the food.

"Okay, let's start with the 'bigger isn't always better' notion," Harlan said.

"The opinions reflected here are not necessarily those of the person speaking," Jonas grinned at his boss. "Right?"

"Right! We're just debating the issue. Go for it."

"Okay," Jonas took a bite of Lynne's excellent Mexican casserole. "Seems like when people get bigger with their farms, it's easier to go into debt. They always want a little more—they're never satisfied. We're taught to be satisfied with our station in life."

Chapter
7

"But can't a person be satisfied and still be progressive? Satisfied is one thing—not being able to support your family is another."

"You're assuming we won't be able to support our families while using horses. We have—we are—now."

"Yes, but you know what else? Families are depending a lot on their teenagers to bring in money. That puts the teens out in the world and exposes them to all kinds of temptations—like modern farm equipment, cars, and of course worldly girls and boys!" Harlan grinned at Jonas. "Isn't that right?"

"True. But having tractors won't change that."

"Maybe then the kids and the mothers wouldn't have to help bring in money. Is it my imagination, or are there more Amish women with jobs these days? You know, housecleaning, the restaurant, bakery—that kind of thing."

"I don't know. For sure they stay home when they have young children. They don't take jobs and have somebody else raise their kids. They don't believe in that."

"So tell me, Mr. Young Amishman, when you have a wife and five children under school age, how are you going to feed and clothe them?"

"I plan to be working for the best dairy in the county—who knows—I might even have had a raise or two by then!" Jonas's blue eyes teased Harlan. "I'll have my own dairy cows, so we'll have all the milk we need. My wife will grow a lot of our food, and we'll have chickens for eggs. We'll butcher a steer, a pig, and chickens now and then. Clothes are much cheaper if they're homemade rather than store-bought, and if the kids are as close together as you predict, we'll just keep using the same clothes! We can burn wood that I cut from our land. Think about the bills you have. Electricity, car payment, heating and air-conditioning, tele-phone, credit cards—we won't have any of those. The investment and upkeep of my horses will be a lot less than your tractors," Jonas paused, almost surprised at himself. "Does that answer your question?"

Harlan laughed—a hearty, good-natured laugh that invited a chuckle from Jonas too. "Sounds to me like you've got it all fig-ured out!" Harlan said. "But for the sake of our little discussion here, tell me this: Is there actually something wrong with tractors, or is it just the idea of progressing forward?"

Chapter
7

Jonas didn't respond as he buttered a second piece of bread and took a bite. When he answered, his words were much slower and more reserved than before. "My dad would say it's the idea. Today we decide to have tractors. What will we do 20 years from now? And 20 years from then? When would it end? Our simple lifestyle is part of us. It's both what we do and who we are."

Jonas had been tracing the tablecloth pattern with his tooth-pick as he spoke. The tracing continued after his words stopped, and Harlan didn't ask any more questions.

❖ ❖ ❖

The propane lamps in the Bontrager house had been burning for an hour already when Jonas arrived at home that evening. That was the other thing he didn't like about winter, Jonas thought as he parked the truck under the trees. It was dark in the morning when he left and dark when he came home. On the pos-itive side, he knew the house would be warm. The wood heat com-bined with the warmth thrown by the lamps made for a cozy house. He didn't mind spending winter evenings with his family during the week. By the time supper was eaten and the dishes done, there wasn't that much time before everyone went to bed around 9:00. Time enough for a game or two with his brothers and sisters, or to read the newspaper.

"I have something for you," Roseanne said quietly to Jonas

as they dried dishes together. It was the twins' turn to wash, and they were making a party of it. Roseanne was constantly telling them to stop splashing water on each other.

"What?" Jonas wondered.

"You got a letter in the mail today."

"Really? Who from?"

"Well, the return address is Florida."

Jonas's heart jumped.

"Where is it?"

"In my room."

Jonas threw his towel on the counter, grabbed a flashlight lying nearby, and sprinted toward the stairs. Roseanne followed, and two sets of feet raced up the stairs to her room. Jonas flung open the door and searched the top of Roseanne's desk, vanity, and dresser with the flashlight beam. "Where is it?" he repeated.

"Patience, my brother, patience," Roseanne chided. "I hid it so the other kids wouldn't see you got it. They'd never leave you alone." She opened the top drawer of her vanity and took out a light pink envelope. "Even smells good," she put it to her nose and then handed the envelope to Jonas.

"Thanks," he said, and was gone.

❖ ❖ ❖

Jonas lit the small lamp on his bedstand, and sat down on the sagging old double bed. The pink envelope in his hand did smell good. Sweet. Feminine.

Dear Jonas, his eyes devoured the words.

Thought I'd write and let you know how we're doing down here. We're having a great time. I got a job in a grocery store. Right now I'm carrying groceries out, but I might be able to move up to being a cashier.

Of course carrying groceries out here is sheer pleasure, because the weather is so nice. I bet you're freezing your butts off there. Don't you wish you'd come along?

We haven't done too much so far other than get jobs and places to live. I'm in an apartment with two other Amish girls from Indiana. It's kinda bare because we didn't bring anything with us and so far haven't bought much. At least it had furniture. The people here are used to Amish kids showing up and needing a furnished apartment, so they're available, although more expensive than other apartments.

We've been to the beach a few times. The ocean is so endless! I don't know what I expected, but it's a lot of water compared to what we see in Kansas! It's cool the way the tide comes in and goes out. The smell, the sand, the sea-gulls—it's all so different. We've been in the water a little bit—that was fun! Some of the guys tried body surfing. The most I've done was let a wave lift and carry me a little bit. You should try this sometime—you'd love it.

Mom wrote me about the stuff going on back there with people wanting to get tractors. I guess Dad's one of them. Your dad's on the side of staying with horses, isn't he? Sounds like this could be a big deal before it's all over. I don't know what I think—it seems far removed from me while I'm here. Have you gotten caught up in the argument?

Well, I don't know what else to say. Why don't you surprise me and pick me up after work sometime, like you did at the restaurant? I usually work the 3:00-10:00 shift at the Sunset Market right on Main Street. You can't miss it.

I miss you.
Bye!
Sue Ann

Jonas laid across the bed for a few minutes, then sat up and read the letter again. Her parents and his parents were on opposite sides of the controversy. She said she missed him. She said she'd like for him to come see her. How he'd love to do that. And how he hated this tractor stuff.

Chapter
7

Chapter 8

Christmas

"Jonas, get up! Time to chore!" The words penetrated Jonas's dream—a dream he really didn't want to leave behind. He didn't want to wake up. He and Sue Ann were lying on the beach together....

"It's Christmas! We need to chore and go to Dawdi's," his brother Robert's excited voice insisted. "Come on!" Jonas felt the covers being pulled away from his body, and he knew the dream was over. He snatched the covers back, mumbled something to Robert, then slowly sat up in the bed. The room was cold and dark. It was still pitch black outside the window. He'd give anything to be living his dream, soaking up the warm Florida sunshine with Sue Ann.

But no. No, he was in Kansas. A full day of eating, games, gift exchange, and visiting with his relatives lay ahead. He'd better get with the program.

Like winter versions of summertime fireflies, the lights of flashlights dotted the Bontrager yard when Jonas stepped out of the house with a Coleman lantern in his hand. Each of his five siblings had morning chores to do, and each had to carry a light. Jonas could hear the diesel motor of the milking machine running, and the early morning call of the roosters. It was shortly after 5:00, and they'd probably been at it for an hour already. He never could understand the time clocks on roosters, he thought.

Jonas heard a meow and felt a bump on his ankle. His lantern caught a large reddish-orange cat in its circle of light. "Merry

Christmas, Red," Jonas bent down and scooped the cat up in his free arm. The cat reached up to Jonas's shoulder with his front paws and began rubbing his head against Jonas's neck. "Your motor's going strong this morning too," Jonas told the cat. "Let's go see if we can find you some milk."

Jonas spent the next two hours helping his father and Roseanne milk the cows. His mother and the other siblings pitched hay into the feedbunks for the dairy herd, horses, and sheep; gave the young calves their milk; and carried feed and water to the farm's chickens and pigs. Robert and Rebecca took care of their pet rabbits and doves, and then ran inside to clean up and get ready to go. They could hardly wait.

❖ ❖ ❖

"It's been a long time since we were all in this surrey together," Esther smiled, looking around at her six children squeezed into the two-seated buggy.

"I think we've grown a lot since then," Jonas commented from the bottom row in the back seat. "Roseanne sure seems to take up more space than she used to. Especially in the hip area, if you know what I mean."

"It's not me," Roseanne retorted. "It's David here next to me. Too many cookies."

"Can't be David," Robert said from David's lap. "His bony knees are killing me."

"Children, children," Esther reprimanded. "Let's sing. How about 'Silent Night'?"

And so the Bontragers sang their way to the home of Esther's parents. With the cloth sliding doors pulled down on the sides, the window down in front and latched tight, and the body heat of eight people inside, the buggy was almost cozy. "Good thing May knows her way to Dawdi's," Fred commented. "I can't see a thing through this window. Too much hot air in here."

May did know her way, and as the Bontrager surrey neared

the farmstead, the horse began to slow down. A brief instruction from Fred through the driving reins, and she was standing in the lane, waiting for the family to unload.

The smells of turkey, dressing, and homemade rolls met Jonas as he stepped inside the door to his grandparents' house. This would be a fun day. In addition to all the good food, he'd enjoy being with his cousins—ranging from little Letha, the toddler, to Lyndon, who was just a year younger than Jonas. They'd exchange gifts, play games, and eat candy all afternoon. Yes, it felt good to be there.

"Betcha you draw washing dishes," Lyndon greeted him with a reminder of the family Christmas tradition.

"Not a chance," Jonas playfully pushed his cousin's shoulder. "It's your turn. You, or one of the girls. They usually get it anyway."

The "norm" at family gatherings was always that the women prepared the food and washed the dishes, but that changed at Christmas. Once a year the women might be able to get out of the kitchen. It all depended on the luck of the draw.

"I'm ready for the couch," Fred said, leaning back in his chair and rubbing his stomach an hour later. "Gotta let this settle so I can put some more in."

"You know better, Dad!" Roseanne challenged. "It's time for the drawing!"

Roseanne jumped up from her seat and went to the kitchen where a peanut-butter bucket stood on the counter. Shaking it on her way to the large dining room table, she explained, "We'll draw one at a time and you'll read what yours says." She removed the lid from the bucket and held it up in front of Grandpa Yoder. "You first, Dawdi."

"You know I can't see very good for washing dishes," the tall elderly man with the long white beard said. "We wouldn't want dirty dishes now, would we?" He slowly reached into the bucket, drew out a slip of paper, and opened it. "Wipe the little children's faces," he read.

"No problem," he added. "I can do that by feel if I have to."

The bucket made its way around the table, with everyone over the age of 12 taking a piece of paper and revealing their assignment. Cheers and good-natured bantering followed each announcement, along with grins of relief or frowns of disappointment from the one who'd just drawn. By the time the bucket got to Lyndon, no one had drawn "washing dishes." Lyndon smirked at Jonas seated beside him and picked out a paper. He read the slip, then quickly put it in his pocket.

Chapter
8

"Read it! Read it!" echoed around the table.

Lyndon rescued the slip from his pocket, opened it dramatically, and with more than a hint of gloating in his voice read, "Take the slop out to the dogs and cats."

Jonas groaned out loud. Lyndon had escaped, and he was up next. Fishing around in the bucket, he took a paper out, then looked around the table. Everyone's eyes were on him, and everyone was smiling.

Jonas opened the paper, took one look at the two words, stuffed it in his mouth and swallowed.

"He's washing dishes! He's washing dishes!" Jonas's twin brother and sister chorused.

"What's the matter, you didn't have enough to eat? You have to eat paper?" Lyndon nudged Jonas. "I'll be carrying the slop out. You're welcome to pick through it before it goes to the dogs."

Jonas made a face at him—at the family in general—and the bucket continued around the table. Roseanne was the last to draw. She took the remaining slip out and read "Sweep the floor."

During the next half hour, as family members went about their assigned tasks, a few ornery ones took it upon themselves to tear used napkins onto the floor. "Gotta make sure you have something to do," Robert explained to his sister when she gave him a dirty look.

❖ ❖ ❖

Like other Amish houses, the home of Grandpa and

Grandma Yoder didn't look any more like Christmas than it did in July. No Christmas tree, no decorations. The only sign of Christmas was the string of Christmas cards hanging along one wall, and the pile of gifts between the bed and the wall in their bedroom. After the dishes were washed, the floor swept, and everything back in order, the family gathered in the large living room to exchange gifts.

Letha, the youngest, began the gift exchange by handing hers to the person whose name she had. That person then continued the cycle. After Dawdi opened his gift—a warm winter coat made by one of his daughters-in-law—he stood up and slowly walked to Fred. Standing in front of his son-in-law, he explained, "You'll have to go to the barn to get your present. You might need this key." Taking a key out of his pocket and handing it to Fred, he shuffled back to his chair.

"What could it be that needs a key?" Rebecca wondered, then giggled at her inadvertent rhyme. She skipped across the room to where her father was sitting. "I'll go along to see!"

"Come along, you little rhyming girl," Fred stood up and walked toward the door. "What could it be? It beats me!" he glanced at his father-in-law, who just smiled.

Several minutes later, Fred and Rebecca were back in the living room, empty-handed except for a small piece of paper in Rebecca's hand. "Tell them what we found," Fred told his daughter.

"Well, we went out to the barn," Rebecca said, feeling very important to have the attention of the whole group. "We looked around but we couldn't see anything that looked like a present. Then we saw a piece of paper tied to the team harness," she paused, looking at her father for reassurance. He winked and nodded. "Here's what it says," she continued, holding up the note.

"Fred: As I plan to have farm sale soon and retire from farming, I won't need my six-horse harness anymore. I know you could use a good working harness. I'd rather you have it than put it through the auction. Merry Christmas! Dad."

Rebecca sat down. For a moment, no one spoke. The gift had caught everyone by surprise. Finally Fred said, "But why the key, Dad?"

The old man smiled and his gray-green eyes laughed under bushy white eyebrows. "I said you *might* need the key. Never said you would."

The children giggled, but most of the adults remained silent. Fred continued, "Thanks, Dad. You know we'll put it to good use, and I'm glad the harness is staying in the family."

Jonas looked at his uncles. Their faces betrayed very little, but the tension in the room was unmistakable. During the recent discussions about buying tractors, Fred was the only son-in-law who had made it clear he would stay with horses. With his gift, Dawdi had powerfully and not-so-subtly supported Fred's stand.

❖ ❖ ❖

"So, did you have a good Christmas?" Debbie queried Jonas the next day as they shared a booth at the local Pizza Hut. Debbie was home from college for Christmas vacation, and she'd asked Jonas if he wanted to run into town for lunch. They'd seen very little of each other since she'd gone to college late in August, and Jonas wondered how she was doing. Besides, she'd offered to buy, and he'd never turn down free pizza.

"Did I have a good Christmas?" he repeated. "Well, if lots of food makes a good Christmas, I did. And I had fun with my cousins. But I had to wash dishes!"

"No! How'd that happen?"

Jonas explained the Christmas ritual to Debbie, who ate up every word.

"That's one thing that's so cool about your family," she said. "You have so much fun together!"

"Yeah, I guess so."

"You sound less than enthusiastic."

"It's kinda weird on that side of the family right now, with the tractor thing going on."

"I've heard just a little bit about it. Tell me."

Jonas explained the situation, and concluded with, "So you can see that when Grandpa gave my Dad a harness to use with horses working in the fields, it was a loaded present."

"No kidding. Where do you fit into this whole thing?"

"I'm not sure."

"Well, you'll have to decide when you join the church, won't you?"

"That depends on what happens between now and then."

"Meaning ..."

"If the church splits, I guess I'd have to decide which one to join. If it doesn't, I don't."

"You think it'll split?"

"I think it might."

"Jonas! Isn't that crazy?"

"Maybe. But your church has had splits too, hasn't it?"

"I suppose so. It just seems like when our church has disagreements, it's over something theological. Whether to use horses or tractors doesn't seem like a theological issue to me."

"What theological issues would your church split over?"

"You know, things like what we believe is right or wrong."

"My dad believes that using tractors would be wrong for him as an Amishman."

"But where in the Bible does it say that?"

"I don't know. I do know it says a woman should keep her head covered," an impish grin spread across Jonas's face. "You're not doing too good in that department."

"That's Paul talking," Debbie countered. "I don't think a woman's salvation is dependent on having her head covered."

"So, Miss Theologian, tell me then, what is salvation? And what is it based upon?"

"John 3:16. 'For God so loved the world, that he gave his only begotten Son, that whosoever believeth in him should not perish, but have everlasting life.' That's it. Plain and simple."

Jonas didn't respond as he concentrated on a piece of pizza. Plain and simple. Those were words used to describe the Amish. The Plain People, living a simple lifestyle. But somehow church stuff had never seemed very simple. Why did it seem so simple to Debbie?

"Jonas," Debbie was talking to him. "Do you think you're a Christian?"

65

Chapter
8

Chapter 9

Letters

Debbie's question bugged Jonas long after he gave her a non-committal answer during their lunch together. Was he a Christian? He'd told her he didn't know. She'd said maybe he needed to think about it. He'd said, "Maybe," and then changed the topic.

As he thought about it during the next few days, he vacillated back and forth. On the one hand, running around and partying with the Amish young folks probably didn't qualify him as a Christian. Yet he didn't get himself into trouble like some of the other kids did, and he kept his drinking in control. He tried to be respectful to his parents. Basically, he was a good kid. So maybe he was a Christian. But he hadn't been baptized and joined the church, and that was probably the real test.

The thought of writing Sue Ann about the topic crossed his mind briefly at one point, but he shrugged it off. They'd corresponded several times since he received her letter early in November, and although they weren't sharing very personal things, Jonas was thrilled just to be hearing from her. A week after his lunch with Debbie, he got a letter from Sue Ann. In addition to her usual questions about what was happening in the Amish community, she'd asked him about Debbie. Had he seen her over Christmas vacation?

Jonas wondered what, if anything, was behind Sue Ann's question. Would she be jealous of his spending time with Debbie? He kind of hoped so. And then he had an idea. He'd tell Sue Ann about his lunch with Debbie. And he'd tell her what Debbie had asked him.

If there was one thing harder than writing a letter, it was finding a time and place to do it. With curious family members all over the house, he couldn't just sit down at the family dining room table one evening and write Sue Ann. No way. His room wasn't a better option, because his curious siblings would be there in no time, wondering what he was doing there by himself. He finally decided to do it one evening after everyone had gone to bed. He'd stay up on the pretense of reading the newspaper, and after everyone was out of the dining room, he'd write Sue Ann.

67

Chapter
9

Roseanne didn't seem in a bit of a hurry to go to bed that evening early in January. She dawdled around in the kitchen for awhile, claiming she was hungry and needed a bedtime snack. Then she brought her milk and cookies into the living room where Jonas sat crosswise on the couch, the newspaper in front of him.

"How many times you gonna read that paper, Jonas?" Roseanne smirked. "Looking for something special?"

"None of your business," he replied, turning the page. "Can't a man even read the paper around this house without getting put on trial?"

"Would you like some milk and cookies while you write—I mean read, your letter—I mean newspaper?" she giggled.

Jonas looked up at his sister standing next to him. She'd seen through his guise, and was going to milk it for all it was worth.

"I can set them on the table here for you—since you'll probably be coming here to do your writing, I mean reading," she could hardly keep her mirth in control. "Hope you don't mind if I join you. I'm gonna read my book and have some cookies too."

Jonas didn't answer. He continued to read the sports page, and when he looked up a few minutes later, Roseanne was sitting at the table, still wearing her silly smile. She'd been watching Jonas, but her eyes quickly dropped to her romance novel when he caught her eye. She munched slowly on a cookie and pretended to be deeply involved in her book.

Jonas got up, rummaged around in the desk for paper and a pen, and sat down on the opposite side of the table from Roseanne. He'd never wait her out, so he might as well begin.

Dear Sue Ann, he wrote. *How's everything in Florida? Not much new here. Cold, but no snow. I thought about you in that warm weather on Christmas Day, and I was wishing I could be there.*

Jonas paused. Was that too forward? He considered starting over. No, he'd leave it.

We had the usual Yoder family get-together on Christmas Day. I had to wash dishes. Not the highlight of my day, but I lived through it. Dawdi gave Dad his six-horse harness as a present. The uncles didn't say anything, but you can imagine what everybody was thinking. Dad's the only one who's dead-set on staying with horses, and the others want tractors.

What do you hear from your folks about this mess?

You asked if I saw Debbie over Christmas vacation. She took me out for pizza one day. I guess it was good to catch up with her, he paused again, chewing on the end of the pen.

We talked about the tractors and horses. She got into one of her religious-talking moods. She asked me the craziest question.

Roseanne stood up and studied her older brother. He seemed lost in thought. She cleared her throat. "Tell Sue Ann hi from me," she teased. "Tell her to come home soon. Tell her my brother is dying for her sweet love and affection," she waited for a reaction from Jonas. When he refused to look up, she made a big show of opening her book and began leafing through the pages. "Let me see if I can find some better, more juicy things to say," she said, then leaned down next to Jonas and pointed to a spot on a page. "How about this?"

Jonas protectively placed his arm over the letter and glared at the face next to his. He wanted to be mad at her, but he really couldn't. Roseanne's cheeks were red from the warmth of the propane lamp, and her blue eyes and impish smile finally elicited a half-smile from him too.

"Just leave your book here," he conceded. "I'll pick my own juicy words."

"If you need to make sure they're the kind of words a girl wants to hear, I'm available," she giggled again. "I'm sworn to secrecy!"

"I'm sure you are," Jonas muttered. "And now, if you don't mind, I have a letter to write."

Roseanne left, and Jonas returned to the page in front of him.

She asked me the craziest question, he'd written. *She asked me if I'm a Christian. Isn't that strange? What would you say to a question like that?*

There, he'd leave it at that.

Roseanne says hi, he continued. *She wanted to help me write this letter. She wanted me to take some stuff out of her trashy love-story book. I don't think so.*

I will repeat one thing Roseanne said. Tell Sue Ann to come home soon, she said. Sounds good to me. Do you have any idea when you'll be heading back this way?

Now came the part where he never knew what to say. After staring at the table for awhile, he concluded:

Love, Jonas.

Lots of people signed letters that way, he rationalized. It could mean nothing, or it could mean everything. Or something in between.

Not much of a letter, he thought, re-reading the page. Oh well, maybe he'd write more next time. He found an envelope, folded the page, and slipped it in. He licked the flap and sealed it. Grabbing a flashlight from the kitchen counter, he turned the knob on the propane lamp until the bright white light slowly died. Flashlight in one hand and envelope in the other, he quietly ascended the stairs to his bedroom.

❖ ❖ ❖

Jonas wouldn't admit it to anyone—barely to himself—but he could hardly wait to get a letter back from Sue Ann. He even calculated the earliest day it might arrive. How long would it take his letter to get to Florida, he wondered. Maybe three days? If she sat down and wrote him the day she got the letter, then another three days back to Kansas. A week. The earliest he could hope to hear from her was in a week.

A week came and went, and no letter. Jonas knew Roseanne was making a point of getting the mail every day. So far, the question in Jonas's eyes when he came home from work had been met by a slight shake of Roseanne's head. Almost two weeks after he wrote Sue Ann, Jonas walked into the house to be met by Roseanne, grinning from ear to ear. "That *newspaper* you stayed up late to read a couple of weeks ago?" she whispered loudly. "They want to know if you want to buy a subscription."

Jonas bolted for the stairs, and Roseanne followed with a laughing scream, "You stay out of my room!"

Reaching her bedroom seconds later, Roseanne and Jonas stood panting and grinning at each other. Neither had brought a light with them, so Jonas ran back down for a flashlight. He held it while Roseanne lit the lamp in her room, then she reached into her desk drawer and took out the pink envelope.

"What's it worth?" she teased.

"What's your life worth?" Jonas grabbed her in a full body squeeze and began to tighten his hold. Roseanne tried to struggle, but he'd caught her by surprise.

"Let ... me ... go ... Jonas!" she giggled, still trying to break away.

"Give me the letter. Or I'll start tickling."

"No!" Roseanne shrieked. "It's getting all crumpled up!"

Jonas released his hold, but not before he got in a good tickling dig in her side. Roseanne jumped away, threatening, "I shouldn't give it to you, just for that."

But she did, and Jonas took the flashlight and letter to his room. He closed the door, lit his lamp, pulled out his pocketknife, and sliced the envelope open. The letter smelled good—just like the others.

Dear Jonas, he read.

Your letter came while I was gone over the weekend, so I didn't get it answered right away. Sorry about that. But guess where we went?

Disneyworld!

Yep, a bunch of us drove down to Orlando and had a great time! You can't imagine what Disneyworld is like. It's huge! We spent two whole days in Disneyworld and Epcot Center—I think we saw most of it, but there's no way we could do all the rides and everything. There's just no way I can describe that place, but I took pictures and I'll show those to you when I come back. I'm glad I went, but believe it or not, it sorta made me appreciate being Amish. It's kinda hard to explain, but I'll try.

For one thing, everything was so expensive. The food, the souvenirs, the ticket to get in—it all cost an arm and a leg. I can't imagine being parents taking a family in there. I guess we Amish are used to finding cheaper ways to have fun.

*Of course they had the latest technology in every-
thing—I didn't understand how they did half of the stuff
they had there. That was fun to see, but it made me realize how much I don't know about the world in general. In
some ways, I felt stupid. But as I've thought about it since
then, I've realized that probably isn't important for me.
What good are all those worldly things if you don't have
a strong family and good friends?*

Jonas paused, digesting what he'd just read. What was Sue
Ann saying? Was she disillusioned with Florida? Was she ready to
come back? He continued reading.

*There are a lot of Amish kids here just messing
around, looking for a good time. Sometimes I get the feeling they're the leftovers from their communities—kids
who are looking for mates because they haven't found
anyone yet, or who just don't know what they want to do
with their lives. They think that partying and hanging
out on the beach and seeing the sights—that's the good
life. It all seems so superficial.*

*Like when you wrote in your last letter about your
talk with Debbie. Nobody talks about that stuff down
here. Especially not the guys. For that matter, I don't
remember guys at home talking about it either. Seems
like one day they're running around and being crazy, and
the next day they're ready to settle down and be Amish.*

*You're different that way, Jonas. You think about
things. I like that.* Jonas stopped and let the words soak
in. He read the last paragraph again, and then went on.

*I don't know what I'd say to Debbie's question if I
were you. She seems awfully interested in your personal
life, asking those kind of questions. I know that because*

you think about those kinds of things more than a lot of other kids, Debbie is somebody to talk to about it. But I'm not sure she's the best person to help you process it.

A pang of defensiveness hit Jonas. What right did Sue Ann have to tell him who to talk to? At the same time, he remembered the times he and Sue Ann had talked about "heavies." Both of the girls pushed his thought processes, in different ways. And without coming right out and saying it, they were jealous of each other. What do you know, two women jealous of each other over him. Jonas smiled.

Mom's written about the tractor thing, Sue Ann changed the topic abruptly. *She's afraid there's going to be a split in the church. She says Dad's been looking at tractors at farm sales and in town already, and he's not the only one. Looks like I may be coming back in time to see the church divide. That would be awful.*

About when I'll be coming back. It sorta depends on when I can catch a ride. I'm guessing it'll be sometime in March or April. In the meantime, go ahead and send some of those sexy words from Roseanne's romance novel. Or make up your own!

Personally, I don't need to read a book. I just think about that good-looking guy in the black cowboy hat that took me to Garth Brooks....

Love, Sue Ann

A rush swept through Jonas, and he read the last sentence again and again. Yes. Yes. YES!

Chapter 10

Kisses

"**A**ll right, big guy, let's go!" Jonas instructed his horse, Lightning, slapping the driving reins across the broad brown back. "I've waited long enough for this! Let's fly!"

Lightning sensed the excitement in Jonas's voice and through the reins, and left the Bontrager yard in a fast trot. Barely slowing down for the turn onto the road, the horse's speed tilted the buggy crazily, and Jonas laughed loudly inside the black box.

"Let's go, Lightning!" he exclaimed.

Jonas searched his tape box until he found the one he was looking for—Mary Chapin Carpenter. He popped it into the player, turned up the volume, and sang along with the country musician. "I feel lucky! I feel lucky tonight!"

Did he ever. Sue Ann was home. A perfectly still, beautiful March sunset unfolded in front of him, and the meadowlarks sang from fence posts, heralding spring. Acres of bright green wheat fields lay bursting with potential alongside the road. The wheat looked good this year, and farmers were hoping for a bumper crop.

As Jonas watched, the sun kissed the Kansas countryside with a last touch of gold. The big red ball disappeared, leaving behind streaks of colored clouds sweeping across the sky. A solitary jet stream made its white way across the backdrop of color, and Jonas wondered what it must be like to be up there. He'd never flown, and he probably never would. It didn't really matter. He could live the Amish lifestyle, giving up worldly conveniences, as long as he was sharing his life with someone like Sue Ann.

Their letters had increased in frequency and intensity over the last two months, and Jonas found himself thinking about Sue Ann more and more. Sometimes he wondered how she could possibly like him—surely there had been many opportunities for her to meet guys in Florida. But in her letters, she always talked about her "Amish cowboy in Kansas." Jonas straightened the black cowboy hat on his head, and a twinge of nervous excitement swept his stomach. It'd been almost six months since he'd seen her. He hoped she wouldn't be disappointed.

With its tape player blaring Mary Chapin Carpenter, the buggy careened around the corner of the Eash driveway and up to the house. Lightning stopped at Jonas's command, sweat foaming under the leather of his driving harness and bridle. Breathing hard, he shook his head, then tried to rub it against his leg. He'd paced the four miles between the Bontrager and Eash farms in quick time—now he wanted some relief from the irritating wet sweat under his bridle.

"Lightning! Hold still!" Jonas commanded. He heard the door of the house slam.

Sue Ann was half-running toward the buggy, and the next thing Jonas knew, she was seated next to him. She smelled like the letters she'd been sending. She looked ...

She looked like a dream come true. If she'd been tan before she left, she was darker now. He couldn't see much of the tan, Jonas noted wryly, because she was wearing a prim turquoise blue dress. An immaculate white starched covering hid her long dark hair, but it only accented her face and eyes. The face and eyes he'd missed seeing ... those warm, heart-grabbing dark brown eyes.

Jonas flushed, because he could see her eyes taking him in even as he had absorbed her. Their eyes locked for a moment, then Sue Ann touched his hat and said softly, "Hey cowboy, it's good to see you."

❖ ❖ ❖

They drove into Wellsford to The Deutschland Restaurant for supper. Sue Ann wanted to talk to the manager about getting her job back, and Jonas figured it was a "safer" place to eat than the hamburger joint or Pizza Hut, where they might run into a lot of the young folks. He didn't want to see the other Amish kids tonight. He just wanted to be with Sue Ann.

"So catch me up on all the gossip around here," Sue Ann said as they sat side by side in a corner booth of the restaurant. "Your letters weren't exactly long and packed with news," she teased.

"You know I'm not much of a letter writer," Jonas answered. "You were lucky to get what you did."

"I know I was," Sue Ann agreed. "By the way, did you happen to see anything unusual on our yard when you picked me up?"

Jonas tried to remember. He'd been so excited about seeing Sue Ann ... was there anything out of the ordinary at her home?

"Can't say that I did."

"Dad probably had it parked behind the barn. He bought a new tractor yesterday."

A cold stab hit Jonas. So, the lines had been drawn.

"Really."

"He said if he's gonna do it, he's gonna do it now. So he has it for the fieldwork this spring. He's not the only one. Amos Nisly and Levi Miller did too."

His uncles. Jonas had felt it was inevitable, but the reality still hurt.

"It didn't even come to a vote in the church."

"Dad says there wasn't any point in a vote. Some people are going to do it, and some aren't. I guess there'll be two churches now."

With your family and my family in different churches, Jonas thought.

Their food arrived, and Jonas salted and peppered his chicken fried steak in silence. The evening had started so great. Now this.

"I hate that it happened now, because I was going to start taking catechism when I got back," Sue Ann took a bite of her rainbow trout.

Jonas's fork stopped in midair at the second bombshell. Like the first, he'd expected it. Sometime. But all of these heavy announcements tonight? Why tonight?

"Say something, Jonas. You're being awfully quiet."

"What am I supposed to say? The church is splitting and our families are on opposite sides. You're taking catechism to join the other church. What am I supposed to say? 'See you around'?"

Sue Ann stopped eating, and her hand touched Jonas's leg. She turned to look at him, and her eyes searched his. "I know what you're thinking. It's been bothering me too. I'm sorry I brought it up."

"It's okay," Jonas said, dropping his gaze. "We've got to talk about it sometime."

"Yeah, but not now. Let's have fun now. Tell me about some of the crazy things that have happened with the young folks while I've been gone. Has Edwin gone flying out of a barn lately?"

Jonas chuckled softly. She was right—they needed to switch gears. There'd be other times and places to hash this stuff out. "No, but his horse had kind of the opposite experience a couple of weeks ago."

"What happened?"

"Some guys were racing their horses through a field, and there was an old farmstead with one of those outdoor cellars, you know? It was dark, and they couldn't really see where they were going. Edwin's horse ran over the cellar, except the old wooden door broke under the horse's weight."

"You're kidding! He fell in?"

"Yep. Put that horse right in the cellar. And the buggy with Edwin in it flew over the top."

"Was Edwin hurt? How about the horse?"

"Edwin was fine. The horse was pretty panicked, and they had quite a time getting him out of there. Amazing, but he didn't have any broken legs."

"I can't believe it. Who else but Edwin."

"Yeah, he reminds me a lot of Enos. They were cousins, you know."

Chapter
10

❖ ❖ ❖

A Steve Martin movie was showing in Wellsford, so Jonas and Sue Ann opted for the late show. Something light and hilarious would do them good, they agreed. And although neither of them said anything, both knew that Sue Ann wouldn't be going to very many more movies. As she took the church's instruction class, she would slowly drop the worldly activities and clothing she'd enjoyed since she was 16.

Jonas and Sue Ann emerged from the theater hand in hand after the movie and walked the three blocks to the Star Bowl bowling alley where they'd left Lightning tied to the hitching rack. The Star Bowl was a popular hangout for the Amish young folks, and several generations of Amish kids' horses had spent many hours there. Lightning knew the place well.

Jonas and Sue Ann were in no hurry to get home, so Lightning's pace was considerably slower than when he'd left the Bontrager farm earlier that evening. Jonas held the reins lightly with one hand, his other arm around Sue Ann. She snuggled close, and they drove in silence through the quiet town.

"Well, at least your mom should be glad you went out with a guy driving a horse and buggy," Jonas said quietly in the stillness broken only by the clop-clop-clop of Lightning's shoes on the pavement. The sound reminded Jonas of Sue Ann's mother's comments the previous summer.

"Yeah, that's true."

"Then again, I might be too 'horsey' for your parents now."

Sue Ann didn't respond immediately, and when she did, Jonas heard both determination and frustration in her voice.

"My father got a tractor. I'm going to be baptized in my parents' church. Beyond that, I am old enough to decide who I will date, who I will marry someday, and yes, which church I will be a part of with my husband."

Jonas smiled in the darkness. He dreamed of being that husband. And if that should happen, he knew that he'd have much more than the prettiest young woman in the community. He'd also be hitched for life with a vigorous wife, someone with a mind of her own as well as a strong sense of partnership. If they could just survive the storm between now and then.

Jonas pulled his arm away from Sue Ann and reached into his tape box. In the dimness of the light attached to the outside of the buggy, he found the tape he wanted. He pushed it into the player. Garth Brooks sang "The Dance."

❖ ❖ ❖

"I think I'll miss the music the most," Sue Ann said, seated on her bed thirty minutes later. The light from her lamp cast shadows on the posters of Garth Brooks and Alan Jackson on her walls. A stack of country music magazines occupied the seat of one chair, and Dolly Parton reverberated softly through the CD player's speakers.

"I'll have to sell or give it all away," she continued. "Know anybody who might be interested?"

"I'm sure Roseanne would die for this stuff," Jonas said from his position beside Sue Ann as he flipped through the collection of CDs.

"I'm not ready to get rid of it yet, but the time's coming."

"Yeah, everybody's going to be thrilled to hear you're finally joining," Jonas said, setting the CDs in the bed's headboard. "Even your aunt and uncle in Missouri asked me about you when I was there last fall."

"That's right, you had a date with Naomi that night, didn't you?"

"Yeah."

"I haven't seen her for awhile. Is she pretty?"

"Yeah. Cute, I guess. But Sue Ann," Jonas paused, softly placing one hand on her small waist, the other on her shoulder. "Not half as pretty as you," his eyes met hers. In a heartbeat their lips touched as well, tenderly at first, then stronger and with more insistence as the minutes passed.

Chapter
10

"Let me take my covering off," Sue Ann said finally. "I don't want it to get messed up." She stood up and removed the pins holding the white cap to her head, then set the cap on her dresser. Taking the barrettes out of her hair as well, Sue Ann shook her head, bringing her hair down around her shoulders and back. Jonas watched, and wondered again how he could be so lucky.

❖ ❖ ❖

Jonas woke up long before dawn. In the darkness of the room, it took a few moments before he realized where he was. So it hadn't all been a dream. Sue Ann really was asleep beside him. He'd stayed in Sue Ann's room. People like Debbie and her parents would never believe they'd done no more than some serious kissing before they turned out the lamp and gone to sleep in each other's arms. It didn't really matter what the Schmidts thought, but he did need to be there for milking. He slipped out of the bed, hoping not to wake Sue Ann. Still fully clothed except for his boots, he groped in the blackness, trying to find the door. Sue Ann stirred.

"Jonas?" she whispered.

"Yeah. I need to get going. Gotta be at work."

"Here's a flashlight. Just leave it in the barn when you're done hitching up."

"Thanks," he bent over and kissed her softly. "See ya."

"See ya."

Jonas found his way out of the house and to the barn where

he'd left Lightning five hours earlier. Stepping around the back of the barn, he shone his light around until he saw it—a shiny red International tractor. He turned his attention back to hitching up Lightning to his buggy.

Chapter
10

Chapter 11

"Steady"

Jonas floated through the month of April. As much as he told himself to take things slow and not to rush into anything, he knew he was head over heels in love with Sue Ann. And from all indications, the feeling was definitely mutual.

Even the church split couldn't put a major damper on Jonas's high spirits. Yes, it had happened. The second Sunday in April, Jonas's parents had church in their home. Rumors in the community said that this was the morning the "tractor" people would begin meeting on their own. By 9:30 it was obviously true, because only about half of the families showed up at the Bontragers for church. The other half were at Amos Nisly's home.

Jonas knew the split would affect him. First, he'd have to choose which church to join. Secondly, if he and Sue Ann joined separate churches, and if they got married, they'd need to make that decision all over again as a couple. Those aspects of the future scared him, but for the moment, Jonas couldn't be bothered. For the moment, he was floating above the mess.

And that was his mood the day he saw the trees. He'd gone by them hundreds of times on his way to Wellsford—a group of stalwart cottonwood trees, standing together not far from the road. They were part of a pasture that belonged to his uncle, Amos, and often Jonas would see cattle gathered under the grove of trees. He'd never really thought anything more about them. But that day he did.

❖ ❖ ❖

"So what do you think?" Jonas asked Sue Ann that first Saturday in May.

Chapter
11

Sue Ann looked around, confusion and amusement evident on her face. "I think we're having a picnic in a pasture, and there are some very curious cows keeping an eye on us."

Jonas laughed with delight as he spread a blanket on the ground under a huge cottonwood tree. "It's a great place for a picnic, don't you think?"

"Perfect, absolutely perfect. And the cow pies—they're for dessert?" Sue Ann was laughing now too.

"Hadn't thought about that, actually. No, I think I'd like the whoopie pies in this basket instead."

The couple spread out the meal Jonas had brought—cold chicken, potato salad, homemade bread, slices of cheese, and for dessert—whoopie pies.

"I had no idea you could cook like this," Sue Ann grinned.

"Me neither," Jonas said, scooping a large helping of the potato salad onto his plate. "I had a bit of help from Roseanne."

"It looks great!" Sue Ann bit into a chicken breast, then added, "Now tell me again why we're here?"

"Listen," Jonas said.

A late afternoon breeze was tickling the shiny leaves of the cottonwoods above them. The leaves responded with a soft rustling sound—a sound unlike the wind in any other trees that Jonas had ever heard.

"It's like the trees are laughing," Sue Ann observed. "It's beautiful."

"I've driven by here a million times," Jonas explained. "But the other day it hit me. This would be a perfect place to put a mobile home. I walked around in here one afternoon, and I heard the trees. That did it. What do you think?"

Sue Ann studied her surroundings—the large cottonwoods,

some smaller osage orange trees along a fence row not far away, the spring green pasture, the herd of cows watching from a distance.

"I think it could be nice. Who owns this?"

"Amos Nisly."

"You think you could buy a few acres?"

"I think I'm sure going to try."

"What do your parents say?"

"I haven't told them. I wanted to show you first."

Jonas set his plate of half-eaten food down and took a deep breath. "Sue Ann, I was wondering," he paused, waiting for her eyes to meet his. "I was wondering if you'd like to go steady."

Sue Ann's eyes answered before her mouth verbalized her response.

"Yes, yes I'd like that a lot."

Jonas and Sue Ann knew that, in the tradition of their community, going steady meant much more than it did for the "English" teenagers. For the Amish young folks, going steady was often a pre-engagement time. It didn't always end in marriage, by any means. In fact, Sue Ann had gone steady with Sam several years earlier—a relationship that broke up when Sam decided to leave the Amish. Until now, Jonas had never gone steady with anyone. Now, after turning 20 in April and spending a lot of time with Sue Ann, he knew he was ready.

Jonas leaned over and kissed Sue Ann. "You've made me very happy," he said, allowing himself to get hopelessly lost in her dark eyes. "I'll try very hard to do the same for you."

"You already have, Jonas. You already have."

❖ ❖ ❖

It didn't take long for the word to get out. Jonas and Sue Ann were going steady, and Jonas wanted to move a mobile home into the cottonwood trees along the Wellsford road. Jonas kept waiting for the perfect time to talk to his parents about the plans, but the rumor mill got to them before he did. His father brought it up late one evening after returning from the field with the team of horses. Jonas had just gotten home from the Schmidts, and he helped his father unhitch the team and feed them.

"I hear we're gonna have one less mouth to feed around here," Fred said, pouring grain into the manger for the huge draft horses.

"Uh, yeah, I've been meaning to talk to you about that," Jonas followed his father along the manger. "I'm thinking I'll talk to Uncle Amos about buying the corner of his pasture with the cottonwood trees. I'd move a trailer house in there."

"And why are you thinking about doing this?"

"It's time for me to get out on my own."

"Where you gonna get the money?"

This was the part Jonas had been dreading. He had hoped for a little assistance from his parents. After all, he'd been bringing them his paycheck from Schmidts ever since he started working there four years ago. At the same time, Harlan Schmidt had been giving him calves—a "secret bonus" his father didn't know about. He'd been selling the bull calves and saving the money.

"Well, I didn't know if you'd be able to help or not. Maybe even just co-sign a loan for me?" Jonas asked tentatively. "I've got a little bit saved up. Harlan's given me some calves that I've sold and saved the money."

"Does Debbie have anything to do with you moving out?"

"No!"

"Sue Ann?" Fred set the bucket down and scrutinized Jonas. "Well, yeah."

"You going steady?"

"Yeah."

"You gonna marry her?"

"I hope so." The words slipped out before Jonas could stop them. "I mean, maybe. If she'll have me."

Fred chuckled. "I imagine she'll have you. And yes, if you're going to settle down and be Amish, we'll help you get started. Funny thing is, Harlan was probably hoping his investment in you might lead to a son-in-law for him. Instead, he's helping you buy a home for you to live in and marry Sue Ann. This is good. Very good. Next time I see him, I'll have to thank Harlan for helping you out."

Fred was obviously enjoying the irony of the situation, and Jonas left it at that. He didn't really believe Harlan was helping him out because he wanted a son-in-law. Harlan had told him it was a bonus for his responsibility and hard work. He did the best he could for Harlan, and he appreciated the reward.

"But talking about being a son-in-law," Fred continued. "Sue Ann will have you. But I'm betting Cris and Rachel will have something to say."

"Why?"

"You know why. Because they're 'tractors,' and we're 'horses.'"

"I haven't said which church I'll be in, have I?"

Jonas felt a sudden chill in the air between him and his father, almost as if a cold wind had suddenly blown through the barn door. He wished he hadn't said that. Not now.

When Fred spoke again, controlled anger hung heavy on each word. "You have been brought up working the land with horses. Standing behind a team, close to God's good earth. You have never gone hungry because your father farmed with horses, and your children will never go hungry because you respected the tradition of your family and your religion. God rewards the faithful."

❖ ❖ ❖

Between the long hours of farm work on the Schmidt farm, negotiating the purchase of the land, finding and buying a mobile home, and finally moving it to the land, the month of June flew by for Jonas. Everything had gone much smoother than he could have hoped. For one thing, he'd been afraid Amos might not sell the land to him, since the church split. But his uncle had never mentioned it, and Jonas wondered if it had anything to do with Sue Ann's parents being in the "tractor" church with Amos. He didn't ask, Amos didn't say, and they came to an agreement that worked for both of them.

Finding a mobile home was easier than he'd expected too. A dealer in Vicksburg had a used 14' x 70' that he really wanted to sell. Jonas and Sue Ann borrowed the old '67 pickup and made a trip to Vicksburg to check it out. They agreed that it looked like a good deal.

And so, by the 4th of July holiday, Jonas was living in his own home. He didn't have to worry about telephone and electrical lines being brought in—the only thing he needed was a well.

The evening of the 4th, Jonas and Sue Ann drove his horse and buggy into Wellsford. They hitched Lightning up to his customary spot at the Star Bowl, and then walked to the park where the fireworks would be shown. This was probably one of Sue Ann's last "worldly activities," they realized, because she was in catechism and would be joining the church soon. After the show was over, they walked back to the Star Bowl, talking about how much had happened in their lives since the fateful fireworks show in Vicksburg three years ago.

"Jonas, where's Lightning and the buggy?" Sue Ann asked as they rounded the corner of the Star Bowl.

A pang of panic hit Jonas as he saw the empty spot where they'd left Lightning. "Probably worked himself loose and found some grass to eat around here," he said hopefully, breaking into a run. But a quick check around the Star Bowl failed to turn up a loose horse pulling a buggy.

"He probably went home," Jonas said. "If he doesn't get hit, or tear the buggy up, that's where he'll be."

"Oh I hope so," Sue Ann was near tears. "And what about us?"

"I suppose we could walk to your place," Jonas said. "It's not that far."

"Yeah, we could do that."

Just then a pickup full of Amish guys pulled up at the Star Bowl. "Hey Jonas! You lose something?" Jonas recognized the voice of Edwin coming from somewhere in the bed of the truck.

Jonas and Sue Ann walked over to the truck. They could smell the alcohol on the guys.

"Actually, yes. You happen to see a horse and buggy that belongs to me heading down the road?"

The guys burst into seemingly uncontrollable laughter, slapping their knees and high-fiving each other. Finally Edwin stopped laughing long enough to say, "Yaw, we saw your horse and buggy!" More spasms of laughter. "Come 'ere. We'll give ya a ride."

Sue Ann glanced at Jonas. He knew she didn't want to ride with the guys—he wasn't thrilled about it himself. But it looked like they'd have to.

Surely it was the longest few miles of his life, Jonas thought, scrunched in the pickup bed with Sue Ann on his lap and boisterous guys all around them. They were about to go by Jonas's mobile home when the driver suddenly hit the brakes and made a sharp turn into the lane. As the pickup's lights crossed the yard, Jonas thought he saw the reflective tape of a buggy about 15 feet above the ground. The guys broke into raucous laughter again, and pointed.

Jonas's buggy was on the roof of his mobile home.

Chapter 12

Tornado

"**Y**our horse thinks he's Rudolph!" Edwin roared, standing beside the pickup bed as Jonas and Sue Ann jumped out. "He just went flying up on that roof! Don't know where he is, but looks like he left the buggy up there!"

Jonas had to smile at the sight of his buggy perched on the mobile home roof. It'll be funnier when I know where Lightning is and that he's okay, he thought.

"Where's Lightning?" he asked Edwin. In the darkness, he couldn't see anything other than what the truck's headlights illuminated, and they were pointed straight at the mobile home.

"He prob'ly went down the chimney," Edwin cracked up again. "Right, guys?" he addressed his friends in the truck. "Don't ya think his horse went down the chimney?"

"Yeah, I bet he's standin' in there right now, wondering how he got in that trailer house!" one of the guys agreed, and the whole group exploded. Jonas glanced at Sue Ann beside him. The guys were sure having fun with this! He didn't mind, but he hoped his horse and buggy would survive the trickery of his drunk friends.

"Go ahead, look!" Edwin encouraged. "See if he didn't fall in the chimney!"

"These guys are crazy," Sue Ann whispered to Jonas. "What are we gonna do?"

"I'm not sure. We need to find Lightning, for starters. Let's go in the house and get a flashlight and lantern. They've probably got him tied up someplace out in the trees."

Jonas and Sue Ann walked briskly toward the mobile home, the beam from the pickup spotlighting their way. Jonas opened the door.

"Oh my ... What in the ...!" he exclaimed. "I don't believe it!"

"What is it?" the words were barely out of Sue Ann's mouth before she saw the answer. Lightning stood in the room, filling it with his huge horse presence and aroma.

"Figured we'd give you a housewarming gift!" Edwin yelled from the truck. "You lovebirds have fun!" The truck spun around and roared off the yard, leaving Jonas and Sue Ann in total darkness with a thousand pound horse in the living room.

❖ ❖ ❖

"So what'd you do?" Jonas's brother Robert couldn't believe the story he was hearing. "What'd you do with Lightning?"

"What any sensible guy would do," Jonas stopped eating his scrambled eggs long enough to look into Robert's eyes. "I closed the door on him and said, 'Have a good night, Lightning. See ya in the morning!'"

"You didn't!" Rebecca exclaimed, her eyes big with amazement. "Is Lightning still in your trailer?"

"Jonas, tell them the truth," Sue Ann chided from her spot beside Jonas at the Bontrager table.

"Okay, we led him out and then we walked home."

"And now I need to get home and let my parents know I'm okay," Sue Ann said. "They're probably wondering what happened to me."

"I'm sure they are," Fred agreed. "Do you need a ride home?"

Sue Ann and Jonas exchanged glances, and Jonas answered. "I'll drop her off on my way to work." He nudged Sue Ann. "Maybe when her Mom hears that my buggy is on top of my house, she'll understand why I'm driving her home in the pickup."

"I think it'd be better if I'd take her home," Fred said. "She's joining church. She shouldn't be in that pickup," he paused. "Neither should you, for that matter."

Jonas cringed at Fred's words. Why did he have to make such a big deal out of their driving the pickup? Especially with Sue Ann there. He hated having his parents tell him what to do in front of her.

"I'm driving the truck to work, and her place is on the way. I can drop her off." Jonas hoped the tone in his voice would settle the issue once and for all.

"Suit yourself," Fred stood up from the table. "All I can say is, it's no way to impress Cris and Rachel. And I'd think you'd be concerned about that, if you're goin' steady with their daughter."

"Look, I don't really care how I get home," Sue Ann said. "But Jonas, if you don't mind, maybe it's better if Fred takes me. It keeps everybody happier."

Everybody except me, Jonas stewed. Whose side was she on anyway?

"Fine. Whatever," he pushed his chair back from the table. "I've gotta get to work."

"How're you gettin' the buggy down?" Orie, 13, asked. "Shall me and David come help you?"

"Sure," Jonas said. "We'd better get it down so I can be an *acceptable man* to date Sue Ann. Round up some other guys and meet me there after milking tonight. Bring some good strong ropes along."

❖ ❖ ❖

Jonas fumed all the way to the Schmidt dairy that morning. It wasn't his fault his buggy was on the top of his house. He'd taken it all in stride and enjoyed the joke. Until Fred, and then Sue Ann, had to get involved. A guy couldn't even take his girl home if he wanted to. Ridiculous.

Apologizing for being late, Jonas told Harlan about the

events of the previous night. He left out the part about taking Sue Ann home, even though he knew Harlan would commiserate with him. He just didn't want to talk about it anymore.

"I remember shivareeing new couples that were going steady when I ran around with your dad," Harlan grinned at Jonas. "We might have put a buggy or two on a house, but a *horse* in a *house*—that's a new one!" Harlan leaned against the white milk barn and chuckled. "I hope he didn't leave too much of a mess!"

Chapter
12

"I haven't seen the house in daylight yet!" Jonas grimaced. "I'm going there tonight after chores—if you don't have any field work that needs to be done."

"That's fine. I'd like for you to spend the day working some fields because the weather forecast is for rain tonight. In fact, they're saying there's a good chance for storms."

Later that afternoon, Jonas turned the radio on in the old white pickup as he drove from the Schmidts to his mobile home. True to the predictions, the weather had been strange all afternoon—that hot, heavy "there's a storm brewing" feeling that Kansans came to recognize as "tornado weather." According to the radio, most of the state was under a tornado watch as issued by the National Weather Service. That meant the conditions were right for the possible formation of tornadoes, but there were no threatening conditions at the moment. A tornado watch told the public to keep its eyes and ears open, but to go about business as usual.

That's what Jonas intended to do. Except that it wasn't really business as usual, this matter of getting a buggy down from a roof. He parked the pickup under one of the large cottonwood trees. He couldn't do much with the buggy until his brothers arrived with their ropes, so he might as well go in the house and see what kind of damage Lightning had left.

Fortunately, Jonas had very little furniture in the mobile home. Also fortunate was the fact that Lightning wasn't a very high-strung horse. He apparently hadn't minded being in the house too much. Probably thought it was just another barn, Jonas surmised. Smells like one now too. Good thing we have to take the carpet out anyway, since we don't have electricity to run a vacuum. We'll put new linoleum in, and no one will ever know this was a temporary horse stall. But right now, I need a shovel. Maybe there's one in the back of the pickup.

Jonas stepped outside. A huge dark blue bank of clouds in the southwest grabbed his attention. Doesn't look good, he thought, a queasy feeling growing in the pit of his stomach. Better check the weather on the pickup radio.

The normally bad radio reception in the old truck was nothing compared to what he was getting now. "Tornado warning ... Buffalo ..." he made out amidst the static. "Funnel ... Locust Grove ... Persons ... take cover ... This ... Warning."

A shiver streaked through Jonas and his heart jumped. Buffalo. Their county. Locust Grove was ten miles southwest. Tornadoes usually traveled northeast. He—his family—stood directly in this one's path.

And a mobile home is the last place to be in a tornado, Jonas thought, his hands shaking as he turned the ignition key. A truck isn't any better. Surely he could make it home ...

Jonas gunned the dilapidated pickup onto the road, his eyes riveted to the ominous clouds before him. Pushing the accelerator to the floor, he prayed he could outrace the storm.

Less than a mile from his parents' farm, he saw it. A large gray-black funnel dropped from the cloud bank and Jonas's mouth went dry with horror as he witnessed the churning, spinning motion of the tornado eating its way across the landscape. Spitting out everything it inhaled, the massive windstorm fascinated, even as it terrified him.

"... heading straight ... Amish community ..." the radio crackled. "... take cover ... warning ..."

Warning indeed! Jonas's knuckles gripped the steering wheel. Without radios and televisions, the Amish didn't have the weather information available to them that their English neigh-

bors depended upon. All the extra-sensitive Doppler radar equipment in the world didn't help the Amish. They relied on intuition and weather-sense passed on from generation to generation. Was his family in the basement? Sue Ann?

Jonas slid the pickup onto the farmyard and flew out of the cab. "Tornado! Tornado!" he screamed, sprinting toward the house. The flailing, roaring trees made him wonder if the tornado was already upon them. Reaching the door, he almost ran into his father.

"Dad! Tornado!" he gasped.

"I know," Fred said, his eyes glued to the moving cloud. "I figure it's about a mile away. Maybe it'll miss us."

"If it doesn't, I don't want to be standing here," Jonas panted, unable to squelch the terror in his voice. "C'mon, let's go!"

"Yeah. Okay." Fred seemed almost reluctant, then followed Jonas into the house and down the basement stairs.

"Jonas! You're here!" Relief flooded Esther's voice. "I was so worried about you!"

"Is it coming here?" Rebecca cried. "Are we gonna die?"

"It's okay, it's okay," Roseanne held her sister close. "Sh..sh..sh."

In the light of a flashlight David was holding, Jonas could see his family huddled together in the corner of the basement. The boys wanted to be brave, but he could see them shaking. Roseanne looked terrified too, but she was trying to be strong for Rebecca.

"Fred, what's happening?" Esther asked.

"It was about a mile away, I think."

The noise outside seemed to increase in pitch. Was that the freight train sound people talked about who'd heard tornadoes? Jonas wondered. Any minute now, the house would go ...

"Cover your heads with your hands," Jonas instructed. "Just like they taught you in school." A strange calmness came over him. They had to prepare for the worst. At least he wasn't out alone on the road.

The wild noises of wind and hail continued above them, and

the family waited. Rebecca sobbed softly.

Finally, Fred couldn't take it any longer. "I'm going to look," he said.

"No! It might still be coming!" Esther pleaded.

"It would have hit by now," Fred stated.

"I'm going too," Jonas said, standing up. "I think it missed us."

Fred and Jonas climbed the stairs and walked to the door. Jonas was almost afraid to look out. The yard, though littered with tree branches and hailstones, was basically intact. A rush of relief swept through him. They'd been spared.

"It's okay to come up," Jonas called down to the basement.

❖ ❖ ❖

"I'm going to go see if the neighbors are okay," Jonas told Fred a few minutes later. "I'll take David and Orie with me."

Maybe he won't say anything about the pickup now, Jonas hoped. Maybe it'll be okay because it'll get me there quicker. He considered asking Fred if he wanted to go along, but he knew the answer. His father would never ride with him in a vehicle.

Jonas and his brothers soon saw how close the tornado had come to devastating their farm. Just a half mile down the road, a line of osage orange trees lay twisted and mangled in the ditch. Commonly called "hedge trees," they had been planted years ago along roads and half-mile lines to slow down the wind erosion across miles and miles of Kansas soil. Today, they'd met a monster wind that was more than their match.

The storm had passed, and a soft stillness blanketed the countryside as Jonas continued down the road. The rays of the setting sun cast a golden tint on the world—a world that seemed to have come through the tornado much better than Jonas expected. Pushing its way almost straight north, the storm had run parallel to the road and spent much of its energy in open fields and pastures. Then, for some reason, it had veered to the right and across the road …

"Oh no!" Jonas cried out involuntarily. "No!"

"Jonas! Your trailer house is gone!" David exclaimed at the same time. "Look!"

Jonas was looking. What else could he do. He gulped. He hadn't been spared after all. The mobile home was definitely gone. In pieces. Scattered throughout the pasture. The only thing left standing was the toilet—a white incongruity in the destruction around it.

The buggy. What about his buggy? He couldn't see it anywhere.

But the loss of his mobile home and buggy wasn't the worst. The worst was the reason he'd fallen in love with this piece of Kansas prairie. The worst was the trees. The stately whispering cottonwood grove now lay in jagged ruins. Trees that an hour ago stood tall and strong, offering protection from wind and sun, now cried out helplessly in the dusk, devastated limbs raised in the surrender of death.

"I'm gonna go look around a little," Jonas told his brothers, his voice breaking.

The Day After

" **I** can't believe all of the people here," Sue Ann remarked as she and Jonas stood together in the middle of what was once his mobile home the morning after the tornado.

"I know," Jonas agreed, picking something up from the ground. "Our families, neighbors, even the Schmidts. There're almost more people here than there is a mess to clean up," he studied the object in his hand. "Garth Brooks. Must've come out of the buggy."

"Have you found the buggy?"

"Last night I looked around a little, but it was getting dark. I found pieces from it, and one wheel. That's all."

"I'm just so thankful you weren't here," Sue Ann moved closer and reached for Jonas's hand. "I don't know what I would've done if something had happened to you."

"Yeah, it's good I left," Jonas agreed. "But you know, I'd been okay if I'd stayed."

"What makes you think that?"

Jonas stepped around the debris until he was standing next to the intact toilet. "Cause they always say the place to go in a mobile home if you're in a tornado is the bathroom. I never knew why that was supposed to be a safe place. But now I have proof," he tapped the toilet tank and chuckled. "Here you have your basic tornado-proof toilet."

Sue Ann giggled. "Very funny, Jonas. We can laugh now, but

I'm still glad you weren't sitting on that toilet when the rest of the house left!"

"Jonas!" Fred called from where he was cleaning up the cottonwood trees. "What shall we do with the trees?"

"What do you mean?" Jonas asked, walking toward his father.

Chapter 13

"Some of them might green out again, I don't know. Those that are ruined, shall we cut them completely down? Leave trunks? Stumps? What do you want out here?"

What did he want? He wanted the trees back.

"I don't know," he answered. "For now, let's just clean up what's on the ground and trim the broken limbs from the trees," he surveyed the destruction. "Who knows if I'll even live here," he added, half to himself.

"What do you mean, 'if you'll even live here,'?" Sue Ann inquired from behind Jonas. He turned to see the questions in her dark brown eyes.

"You know I chose this place because of the trees," he said, turning away so Fred and the others cleaning up wouldn't hear him. "It's not the same now."

"No, it's not the same. And I've never pictured you as a quitter," Sue Ann replied.

Surprised at the edge in her voice, Jonas's brow furrowed as he tried to read her face. "What do you mean, 'a quitter'?"

"We'll talk about it later. We have cleaning up to do right now."

❖ ❖ ❖

By late morning, the work was done. Several large piles of wood from the trees and mobile home were burning. Another stack of debris awaited transport to the county landfill. The group of forty-some Amish men, women, and children planned to move on to another farm that had received damage, but first they'd eat the picnic lunches they'd brought along with them. Jonas realized again how much he missed the trees. Without them, there was no shade from the blistering July sun. Most of the workers retreated to the hedge trees, which hadn't been hit.

"Where shall we sit?" Jonas asked Sue Ann, surveying the small groups of people scattered near the trees. The question weighed heavier than it would have a few months ago, because the clusters of Amish people had divided themselves according to the "tractors" and the "horses." Although both groups were there to show their concern and to help with the cleanup, it was obvious that the goodwill didn't stretch far enough to enjoy each other's company while eating. The rift in the church ran deep.

Chapter
13

"Looks like Harlan is keeping your dad busy," Sue Ann noted. "Let's go sit with my folks."

Jonas followed Sue Ann to the blanket her parents were sharing with their three other daughters. He was nervous, but he knew it was a good idea to spend lunch with Sue Ann's parents. He didn't really know them, and well, maybe it was time he made an effort.

"Please join us," Cris invited. "Find yourself a corner of the blanket and have a seat."

"Thanks," Jonas said, feeling the eyes of Sue Ann's mother and sisters watching his every move. "Feels good to sit down."

"Sorry about your place," the stocky man with the thick brown beard said, biting into a ham and cheese sandwich. "You were just getting started, and now you have to start all over again."

"Yeah," Jonas agreed. His sandwich looked identical to Cris's. Maybe because Sue Ann had made all of their lunches, he smiled to himself as he took a bite. He wished Sue Ann and her sisters and mother would talk about something. Why did they all have to sit silently and listen to him and Cris?

"We were talking, some of the other men and me," Cris continued. "Thought we might take up an offering to help you out."

Jonas didn't know what to say. The "tractor" people would

take up an offering for him? Why?

"I really don't expect any money from anybody," he said.

"Other thing is, and I haven't even mentioned this to Rachel or Sue Ann," Cris nodded in the direction of his wife and oldest daughter. "I've got some land you might want to look at. It has big trees on it, and a hedge row along the north side. Make a nice little place to live."

Jonas glanced at Sue Ann. The surprise on her face matched his own. What was going on here? He looked up at Cris. There was no mistaking the open, friendly smile on his face.

"That's mighty kind of you," Jonas replied. "I really haven't had time to think about what I'll do next."

"No hurry on my part. Just keep it in mind," Cris closed the subject as nonchalantly as he'd opened it.

❖ ❖ ❖

Leon Miller, who owned Miller's Buggy Shop in Wellsford, offered Jonas a second-hand buggy to use until he got his own. Following on the heels of Cris's talk about taking up an offering and the mention of a building site on his land, Jonas didn't quite know how to handle it all. He wasn't accustomed to receiving gifts of kindness like that, although he realized it was part of being a victim of the tornado. People wanted to help, and he'd have to accept it graciously. Someday I'll pay them back, he resolved.

Late that afternoon, after helping clean up at several other farms with tornado damage, Fred and Jonas took the team of horses into town to get the buggy from Miller's Buggy Shop. It'd been a long time since Jonas had been alone in a wagon with his father—in fact, the last time he remembered was more than four years ago, when they'd gone into Wellsford on his 16th birthday to buy his buggy. Later that day, Enos had come over to see his new buggy. Now both Enos and his buggy were gone.

"Saw you eating with the Eashes," Fred broke into Jonas's

thoughts. "That go okay?"

Jonas didn't answer. Should he tell his father what Cris had said?

"Tornado take your hearing, son?"

"No, I was just thinking about what Cris said today."

"Oh?"

"He said some of the men had talked about collecting money to help me out," Jonas paused. "And then he said he had a piece of land I should look at to maybe put a house on."

"Well, well, well, now isn't that interesting. You start going steady with Sue Ann, and suddenly Cris and the 'tractor' church are *so helpful.* Of course you know what's going on, Jonas. Bribery. They want you in their church."

"I kinda figured as much," Jonas admitted. "I'm not sure what to do."

"Well, while you're thinking about it, here are some things to keep in mind. Maybe you've heard, maybe you've been too in love to notice, but some of our church people weren't very thrilled with you buying a mobile home. It's hardly ever been done before, and it's a lot of money to spend on stuff you can't use like carpet and electrical wiring. I co-signed the loan because I was happy to see you settling down and hopefully marrying Amish. Now the trailer house is gone. We don't carry insurance, but we Amish always help each other out. The fact that you aren't baptized and a member of the church means that the bishop and ministers will have to decide whether or not the church will cover the cost of the trailer. If I own it, they probably will, although I think they'll warn me about overstepping the boundaries. If you own it, I doubt they'll help out."

"Both our names are on the loan, but I'm paying for it."

"I know. That's what they'll have to decide."

"I can't believe it has to be so complicated."

"You want to talk about complicated? Then think about how I'd feel if you'd up and leave us now and go get money and land from the 'tractor' church. After I helped you get started here."

The words were different, but the tone and the implications sounded so familiar. He could still hear his father saying four years ago, "If you'd end up marrying outside the Amish and leave, it would break my heart." Now even marrying Amish didn't seem to be good enough.

❖ ❖ ❖

As soon as Jonas and Fred returned from Wellsford with the buggy, Jonas hitched Lightning up and left. He had to get away. Too much had happened in the last 24 hours. Too much to think about. He needed to talk to Sue Ann. He needed to hold her.

Sue Ann was working in the garden with her sisters when Jonas turned Lightning into their yard. Along with the wind and small hail, the storm the night before had brought a refreshing rain to crops and gardens. Jonas had never seen Sue Ann be anything but light on her feet, but tonight she was plodding like a draft horse. Her bare tan feet sank into the garden mud with each step, and Jonas couldn't help but laugh from his perch on the buggy seat. Sue Ann heard his chuckle and saw him watching her. Picking a tomato out of her bucket, she took aim and let it fly. It exploded on the seat behind Jonas.

"Hey!" Jonas yelled, jumping down from the buggy. He spotted a nearby watering can, grabbed it, and headed for Sue Ann. Catching her around the waist with one strong arm, he poured the water over his squirming, screaming captive. "Girls! Help me!" Sue Ann yelled at her sisters.

They didn't need a second invitation. The three girls ran for the water hose, and before Jonas knew what was happening, he was soaked. And so was Sue Ann, because Jonas still held her tightly, now with both arms. "Help me get them!" he exclaimed, his dripping face touching hers. "You grab Emma. I'll get Lydi and the hose."

With one lunge, Jonas released Sue Ann and ran for 16-year-old Lydi, who was still aiming the stream of water at them. Jonas's quickness caught her off guard. She dropped the hose and started running, but Jonas nailed her with the cold water. Now it was her turn to scream, and she was soon joined by 12-year-old Emma, who was struggling to get away from Sue Ann. "Here's another one needs cooling off!" Sue Ann laughed. "But you don't have to get me in the process!"

"Just hold her then and we'll do a slow soaking," Jonas approached, brandishing the running hose like a weapon. "Emma, Emma, you haven't had your shower for the day?"

Like most Amish youngsters, Emma was strong from helping with chores and farmwork, but she was no match for her older sister and Jonas. Shrieking as Jonas let the cold water run down her back, Emma soon stood in a puddle of water, her lavender dress soaked and dripping.

"Wasn't there another one here?" Jonas looked around.

"Oh, Katie. She's probably inside," Emma answered. "She's a scaredy cat. Went in to Mommy."

Jonas surveyed the scene. Three soaked girls, their dresses dripping and hugging their slender bodies. His own blue jeans and cotton shirt, equally wet. Sue Ann's bucket lay on the ground, along with most of the tomatoes that had been in it. Dusk was settling over the peaceful farmstead, although a chorus of cicadas made sure the serenity wasn't silent. Fireflies flitted through the yard, and the mosquitoes were out too. He slapped at a mosquito on his bare wet arm as he walked over to where Sue Ann was gathering up her tomatoes.

"Can't say I came over just for a water fight, as much fun as it was," he bent down to pick up the last tomato. "You wanna go into town for some ice cream?"

"Sounds great." Sue Ann stood up, and Jonas's arm found its way around her wet waist as they walked toward the house.

Chapter 14

Decisions

A huge, orange ball full moon sat on the horizon as Jonas and Sue Ann left the Eash yard that evening. The terror of the tornado and emotional trauma of the day seemed to fade into the distance as Jonas relaxed in his borrowed buggy, Sue Ann nestled under his arm. The clop-clop-clop of Lightning's hooves and the song of the cicadas in the trees reminded him of Sunday evenings when, as a child, his whole family went to Dawdi's for ice cream. All six children would be piled in the back of the open wagon, and often they'd sing songs as their parents talked quietly in the single seat in front of them. Sometimes his mother, who had a beautiful voice, would join them, or teach them a new song. He wished he could sing. He enjoyed music, and he could carry a tune, but singing definitely wasn't one of his strong points.

A car approached them from behind, its bright lights illuminating the young couple. As it pulled around to pass, someone yelled from the passenger window, "Hey now! Keep those hands on the reins!"

"Who was that?" Sue Ann asked, leaning forward as the car sped away.

"Didn't know 'em. Just some smart-aleck guys," Jonas answered.

"At least they didn't honk right when they were next to Lightning," Sue Ann said, leaning back into Jonas's shoulder.

"Yeah," Jonas paused, then continued. "I've been wanting to

ask you what you meant about me being a quitter."

Sue Ann didn't answer right away, and when she did, her tone of voice was much softer than Jonas remembered it from that morning.

"When I heard you say you might not go back to your place and start over, I couldn't believe it. It just seemed like you were letting the tornado get the best of you."

"But the trees are practically all gone."

"Maybe a few of them will green out next spring. And you can always plant new trees."

"It's not the same."

"So what are you going to do, look until you find another perfect place with trees? Which brings up something I've been wondering about," Sue Ann slid away a few inches on the seat and scrutinized what little she could see of Jonas's face. "Does my dad know something I don't know?"

"About ..."

"About why is he offering you land to build on?"

"I was going to ask you the same question."

Sue Ann giggled softly. "Seems my dad is making some assumptions about us."

Jonas blushed in the dark and his heart quickened. "I think he is too."

He wanted to say more, but he couldn't. He couldn't tell Sue Ann how he dreamed of making her his wife. He couldn't let her know how he felt he didn't deserve someone so beautiful, so much fun, yet so thoughtful and understanding. He couldn't make himself say the words that found their way into his mind more and more recently—Sue Ann, I love you.

❖ ❖ ❖

A few days after the tornado-accompanied rainstorm, many of the fields in the Wellsford community were in prime condition to be worked in preparation for fall wheat planting. At home,

Jonas's father and siblings kept several teams of horses and mules working long exhausting days. The heat was hard on people and animals alike, but the work needed to be done while the soil was in good condition.

Jonas almost felt guilty leaving early in the morning to milk at the Schmidt dairy, and then spend the remainder of the day in the large John Deere tractor with its air-conditioned cab. While his family toiled away under the merciless sun, he rode in cool comfort, listening to the radio. The incongruity bothered him more than ever before, because he knew he was nearing a point of decision. If he was hoping to marry Sue Ann, he'd have to join the church first. And which church? The "horses" church of his parents, or the "tractor" church of Sue Ann's parents? Either way, someone was going to be very hurt and offended.

And then there was the matter of where to live. Again, he had to choose, and the choice involved saying yes to one family and no to the other.

These decisions weighed heavily on Jonas's mind as he worked in the fields for several days that second week in July. He went through the scenarios over and over again.

If he joined the "horses" church, his parents would be pleased. As a farmer, he would depend upon horses and mules to work the fields. He'd grown up like that and had been driving teams since he was a small boy. But was it viable financially? His dad said yes, the "tractor" people said no.

On the other hand, he understood tractors quite well. Working for Harlan had given him four years of experience driving tractors. He was as much at home on them as he was standing behind a team. He could bring knowledge about tractors to the Amish "tractor" church that few of the men had. Sue Ann's parents would be thrilled, and his, devastated.

Where should he live? The place where his mobile home had been would never be the same, but he was in the process of buying the land. What would he do with that land if he accepted

Cris's offer? Not to mention, how would he deal with his father? Cris's land looked good—it could be the beginning of a beautiful homestead. He yearned for a nice place to share with Sue Ann and hopefully a family someday.

And that was part of the decision too, wasn't it? What would Sue Ann want to do? Shouldn't she be involved in making these choices? But she couldn't until he asked her to marry him, and she said yes.

It was nearing lunch. When he reached the end of the field, Jonas stopped the tractor but left it running. Might as well stay in the air-conditioned cab, he thought. He opened the cooler that Lynne had packed for him and took out a sandwich, chips, apple, and a small bag of chocolate chip cookies. Chocolate chip cookies. They reminded him of Debbie. She used to bring him cookies and ride with him. But they'd started going their separate ways, especially with her making new friends in college and his going steady with Sue Ann.

It would almost have been easier to leave the Amish behind and marry Debbie, he thought. How ironic. If he'd broken away completely, he wouldn't have to make the choices he was facing now. One huge decision, and it would all be over.

Or would it? Would he be able to live with himself if he left the Amish? After all the years of being told by his parents and the ministers that "we are meant to be Amish," could he escape the guilt of defying the religion of his birth?

No, Jonas resolved, that was one decision he'd made, and he was ready to live with it. He was satisfied with being Amish for the rest of his life. And yes, Sue Ann was a big part of that satisfaction.

❖ ❖ ❖

July and August passed. Jonas spent every free moment with Sue Ann. They talked and laughed, teased and tenderly held each other, spending hours together in the blissful state of being in love. Jonas knew, and he knew that Sue Ann knew, they were putting off the big decisions. The piece of land where he'd lived for a few days in his mobile home sat empty. Fred had stopped asking Jonas about it, because the answer Jonas gave was always the same—"It's too hot to build now anyway."

September 11 was Sue Ann's birthday. A week before, Jonas asked Harlan for the 11th off. That morning, an hour and a half before dawn, Jonas hitched up Lightning and left the Bontrager yard at a fast trot. His stomach was in knots, yet he couldn't stop smiling. And Lightning couldn't get to Sue Ann's fast enough.

Reaching the Eash yard, he tied Lightning up at the hitching post, and filled his hand with tomatoes he'd brought from home. Using a small flashlight, he slipped around to the side of the house where Sue Ann's bedroom was. Setting all but one of the tomatoes on the ground, he took careful aim and tossed it at her upstairs window.

Pop. The tomato spattered against the window. Jonas waited, and when nothing happened, he tried again.

Five tomatoes later, Jonas's flashlight revealed Sue Ann's face between the splotches of red on the window. Her dark hair hung down across her shoulders—Jonas had almost forgotten how she looked with her hair down. Now that she was joining church, it was always up under her covering.

The window creaked open. "Jonas!" Sue Ann whispered loudly. "What *are* you doing here?"

"Happy Birthday!" he whispered back. "I came to take you out for breakfast!"

"Well, you could have given me a little warning! Like maybe last night?"

"Uh-uh. Just throw something on and let's go."

"But I look terrible. And I have to put my hair up."

"Nobody's going to see us. Believe me."

"We're going out for breakfast and nobody's going to see us?"

"Right. Trust me. And hurry!"

Jonas didn't know what always took women so long to get ready to go places. Must be a woman thing, he thought. And then he smiled broadly. Something I'll have to get used to.

Sue Ann joined him on the seat of the open buggy. A crisp fall nip hung in the pre-dawn air, and Jonas draped a blanket over their shoulders and laps.

After pulling a buggy in months of sultry heat, Lightning seemed to enjoy the cool, brisk morning, and he paced the few miles to Jonas's destination with his head held high, his senses alert to the world waking up around him.

As they neared Jonas's land where his mobile home had stood, Jonas slowed Lightning down to a walk. The coming dawn illuminated in silhouettes the remaining cottonwood trees. Some were just tall trunks; others still had a few branches. Jonas turned Lightning into the lane and up to one of the tree trunks. Jumping down, he tied the horse up. Grabbing Sue Ann with both hands around her waist as she was about to step down from the buggy, he set her gently on the ground and kissed her. "Happy Birthday," he whispered, and kissed her longingly again.

"Jonas," she said finally. "Maybe we can live on love, but where's this breakfast you promised?"

"Right here, my dear," he said, lifting a picnic basket from the back of the buggy. Throwing the blanket over his shoulder and carrying the basket in one hand, he took Sue Ann's hand and led her toward one of the cottonwood stumps that stood about a foot off the ground. Next to the short stump stood a taller one, and leaning against it was a solitary buggy wheel.

"This wheel," Sue Ann noticed immediately. "Is it from your buggy?"

"Yeah, that's all that's left of my first buggy," Jonas tried to sound casual. "Don't know what I'll do with it—just propped it up there for the time being. Shall we eat?" He laid the blanket on the ground, and opened the basket.

"Fresh cinnamon rolls, compliments of Roseanne," he said,

setting the large soft heavily iced rolls on the tree stump. "And fresh-squeezed orange juice, compliments of me."

"This is so sweet of you, Jonas," Sue Ann enthused. "So romantic!"

"I wanted to be here for the sunrise," Jonas sat down close to Sue Ann. "I wanted to watch it with you on your birthday, and I wanted to ask you a question. But we have to wait for the sun to come up."

"Okay. Shall we eat while we wait? Now that I'm up, I'm starved!"

"Sure!" Jonas laughed.

The young couple sat in silence, watching as the horizon hinted at what was to come, stronger and with more color as the moments passed. When the sun globe slid up, Jonas wrapped his arms around Sue Ann from the back and rested his chin on her shoulders.

"Sun's up," she said, leaning back into his solid chest.

"Yeah. Give it a few more minutes."

Moments passed as the sun rays streamed around them. Jonas wondered if Sue Ann could feel the pounding of his heart against her back. When the world seemed bathed in gold, Jonas took a deep breath and began, "I've been thinking. I'd like to start over again here. And I'd like to plant some flowers—sunflowers—around that buggy wheel. I was wondering if you'd like to plant them with me next spring."

Sue Ann turned her face until their cheeks caressed each other. "Yes, Jonas, I'd love to plant sunflowers with you," she paused. "And if marrying you is part of the deal, I'd love that too."

Jonas felt like whooping, crying, dancing, and flying into the sunrise. Instead, he sat very still and held his wife-to-be as if he'd never let go.

All Things Considered

Unlike newly engaged people "of the world," Jonas and Sue Ann didn't announce their intentions with an engagement ring, newspaper clipping, or even telling their family and friends. The longer they went steady, the more speculation there was in the Amish community about an upcoming wedding, but nobody knew when. They could only talk and watch the signs.

Signs like the new building going up on Jonas's land. Sometime near the end of September, an Amish carpenter crew began working on a square building that, according to passersby, didn't really look like a house. It didn't take long for someone to ask one of the carpenters what that was they were building for Jonas. "A buggy shed," the answer came back.

A buggy shed? The rumor mill chewed on that one for awhile. Why would Jonas build a buggy shed before he even had a house? Did this mean he was going to move another mobile home on that land? Surely not, after what happened to the first one. It wasn't right, that mobile home. Surely Fred would put his foot down before he'd let Jonas make the same mistake again.

And if Jonas and Sue Ann were getting serious, why wasn't he getting baptized? Probably because he and Sue Ann were fighting over which church he should join. Although you'd think, with his working for Harlan and all, he'd be joining the "tractor" church. But then he'd have to face Fred, and Fred was one of the strongest-minded men in the "horses" church. They wouldn't want to be in Jonas's and Sue Ann's shoes right now, no siree. And so the talk went on.

❖ ❖ ❖

"I see you've got yourself a nice little buggy shed out there," Cris Eash commented to Jonas one wet, gray day early in November. The two men happened to be at the blacksmith shop at the same time, getting their horses shod.

"Yeah, now I just need a buggy," Jonas laughed. He knew exactly what Cris was getting at, and he didn't mind stringing him a long a little. If people were so curious, why didn't they just come right out and ask?

"Seems to me you need more than a buggy," Cris continued. "Don't you need a house?"

Jonas chuckled again. The question had probably been driving Cris crazy for several weeks. He'd finally asked it. Jonas noticed that the blacksmith, who'd been hammering a shoe onto Lightning's back left hoof, had paused in midair. He was wanting to hear Jonas's answer too.

"Ah, I figure if it's just me out there, I can live in a corner of the shed," Jonas smiled mischievously. Now Cris would really wonder about Jonas's intentions for his daughter.

"Yaw, I suppose a man living alone doesn't need much more," Cris said, his brown beard moving up and down as he chewed thoughtfully on the end of a pencil. The hammering on Lightning's hoof resumed, and Jonas knew that if he and Cris were alone, Cris just might ask him about his plans for Sue Ann and their home. But not with the blacksmith listening.

❖ ❖ ❖

"It was so funny!" Jonas told Sue Ann that evening as they sat in the Bontrager living room, putting a puzzle together. The rest of the family was gone, so they had the house to themselves. "Your dad was dying to know why I didn't have a house out there, and when I told him I was going to live in the shed, it drove him even crazier. 'Cause of course that's no place for his daughter to move in as a new bride! But he wouldn't say anything."

Sue Ann smiled at the thought of her father and Jonas playing mind games with each other. "They've been asking me too," she said. "They're wondering if there's a certain time they should ask to have church in the spring, 'if we're getting the house ready for something else anyway,'" she giggled. "Maybe we should be thinking about a date."

Jonas didn't answer right away as he studied the puzzle pieces. Something else had to happen soon, if they were going to be married in the spring.

"I'd better start taking catechism," he stated flatly. "Can't say I'm looking forward to that."

"It's not so bad," Sue Ann said, popping a piece into place. The room was quiet for several moments until Sue Ann broke the stillness, "I need to ask you a question."

"Go ahead."

"Are you joining the church because you want to be Amish and live this way of life, or because you know that's the only way you can be with me?"

Jonas didn't answer immediately, then looked at Sue Ann and said, "I'm joining because it is so cool to put a puzzle together on a Saturday night when, if I wasn't Amish, I could be watching college football on my remote-controlled TV."

Sue Ann reached over and grabbed Jonas's cheeks with both hands and pinched. "You are so silly!"

"Ow! Hey! You don't believe me?"

"Just like my favorite thing to do in life is give away all my CDs to Roseanne," Sue Ann responded, "which, by the way, you could take anytime."

"I will. She'll be so excited."

"Now you can answer my question. Seriously."

"Seriously? Seriously I know my happiness in life is related to spending it with you. And I have come to believe that, all things considered, the Amish way is the way for me."

"What do you mean, 'all things considered'?"

"It's the way I want to raise my children. It's simpler and less complicated, most of the time. And it's not worth leaving and disappointing my parents."

"Okay, I buy that. So, which church are you going to join?"

"I don't know. I think we need to talk about that."

"Okay, how about now?"

Jonas sighed and leaned back in his chair. "Maybe you listen in church better than I do. And you're going through catechism. Tell me, where does the Bible tell us what to do when it comes to 'tractors' and 'horses'?"

"I don't think it does. It talks about not being conformed to the world, but that's open to interpretation. Somebody still has to  decide what the boundaries are—where we're getting too worldly."

"And that's the bishop."

"Yes. But the people get to vote too."

"And it takes a 100 percent vote to change anything. You know how hard that is."

"I don't understand it all either, Jonas. Some of it we just accept."

"So how do I decide which church to join?"

"Well, how important are your parents' feelings?"

"I hate having Dad disappointed or mad at me."

"Do you see yourself wanting to farm with tractors?"

"I don't even know if I'll farm for myself. I like working for Harlan."

"I've been thinking about this," Sue Ann took Jonas's hands in hers, her dark eyes searching his face. "If we have children someday, and if I had a choice of them growing up around tractors or horses, I'd choose horses."

"Really? Why?"

"Horses and mules can be unpredictable, I know. Bad accidents happen with them. But tractors seem so big and powerful and dangerous. Maybe that doesn't make sense, but it's how I feel."

Jonas studied their hands entwined together. Should these hands control the steering wheel of a tractor, or work the reins of a team of horses? It might not be either one. But if he had to choose ... if he thought about his sons and daughters ...

Chapter
15

"You know I like horses," Jonas said. "On a good day, I even like mules. I agree. I'd rather have our children grow up with them than with tractors," he paused. "But Sue Ann, it's not that simple!"

"Why not?"

"Because!" Jonas exploded. The trauma of months of internal turmoil boiled to the surface, and Jonas withdrew his hand from hers. "Because our church is divided, our families are on different sides, and we can't just sit here and say we're going with the 'horses' because we like them! It's just not that simple!"

Sue Ann sat quietly, surprised yet not shocked at Jonas's outburst. She studied his face again, now clouded with anger and confusion.

"Maybe sometimes we make things too hard," she said quietly.

Jonas didn't look up, but his mind was spinning. Debbie had said almost the same thing when they talked about religion. He didn't make things more complicated than they were, did he? After all, this was a big decision—which church to join. They had to have good reasons, whatever they did.

"What would we say to your parents?" Jonas asked, half conceding yet half defensive.

"Maybe we tell them we're thinking about the safety of their grandchildren," Sue Ann answered, and Jonas could hear a smile in her voice. "That's a good reason, isn't it?"

"Yes, but they'll still be upset," Jonas said.

"One set of parents will be happy, and one will be hurt no matter what we do," Sue Ann stated. "We have to choose what's right for us and let the chips fall where they may. Don't you think?"

"I guess so," Jonas resigned. Maybe Sue Ann was right.

"When do you want to tell them?"

It was Sue Ann's turn to hesitate, but only for a moment. "Tomorrow's an off Sunday for church. Our families will be home. We can tell yours in the morning and mine in the afternoon."

"Okay. Let's do it."

❖ ❖ ❖

The family was eating a late breakfast when Jonas and Sue Ann came down the stairs together the next morning.

"Morning!" Fred greeted them, his eyes smiling first at Jonas and then Sue Ann. "You're just in time for Mom's fried mush, tomato gravy, and fish!"

"Sounds great," Sue Ann smiled back, taking a chair that young Rebecca had quickly pulled up beside hers.

Sue Ann fit in comfortably with the conversation around the Bontrager table that morning, and after they'd eaten, they all bowed for another prayer. That completed, Fred said, "After the dishes are washed, we'll meet in the living room to read the Bible."

With Amish churches meeting every other Sunday, it was understood that families would read the German Bible together in their homes on the alternating Sundays. This served a dual purpose—to teach the children German, which was different from the Pennsylvania Dutch dialect they spoke, and to acquaint them with the Bible.

"We'll take turns reading from the Gospel of John," Fred said when his family was seated in the living room. "Rebecca, you can start with chapter one."

"But I don't know all the words!" Rebecca complained. "Jonas can start!"

"We'll help you with the words," Fred was firm. "And Jonas will have his turn."

When it was Jonas's time to read, they were ready to begin chapter three. He read the story of Nicodemus, stumbling over some of the German words and paying little attention to the story itself. He continued, and after reading verse 16, a strange feeling of déjàvu hit him. Where had he heard that verse before?

Jonas continued reading, and at the end of the chapter, Sue Ann took over. He heard her voice in the background, but his thoughts and eyes were on the page in front of him.

Chapter
15

"For God so loved the world, that he gave his only begotten Son, that whosoever believeth in him should not perish, but have everlasting life." Those words ...

Debbie! Pizza Hut! That's where he'd heard them before. And the next verse. What did that mean? "For God sent not his Son into the world to condemn the world; but that the world through him might be saved."

So what was all this about God not condemning the world? And what did it mean by "the world through him might be saved." Which world? The "worldly" world the Amish tried to be removed from? What did God want to have to do with that world? Well, he guessed it made sense that the world needed to be saved—whatever that meant. And now he was right back where he and Debbie had left their discussion nearly a year ago. He sighed. Why couldn't anything be easy?

Sue Ann was finished reading, and Fred said the morning's lesson was over. The children scattered, leaving the young couple in the room with Fred and Esther. Jonas looked at Sue Ann, then his parents. "We've decided to get married next spring," he blurted out. "And I'm going to start joining church."

It was Fred and Esther's turn to look at each other, then back at Jonas and Sue Ann. "We're happy for you, and we'd love to have Sue Ann in our family," Esther smiled.

"Which church are you joining?" Fred asked.

"Yours," Jonas answered simply.

Relief evident in his face, Fred continued, "Do your parents know, Sue Ann?"

"No, we'll go over there this afternoon."

"I wish you well."

Chapter 16

Baptism

Jonas warmed his hands over the wood-burning stove in his new buggy shed. The carpenters had divided the building in half with a Sheetrocked, insulated wall. Jonas stood in the "living quarters" half, which also had insulated outside walls. It'll be a nice cozy little place, he thought. We can live here until we get a house. Thank goodness, Cris offered to help with some plumbing, interior walls, shelves, and cabinets.

It had all gone much better with Sue Ann's parents the day before than he'd dreamed. Oh, they'd expressed disappointment that the couple wouldn't be joining their church. But, like Sue Ann had told Jonas later, they were probably thinking they'd rather have her in a more conservative sect of the church than marrying someone like Sam who'd left the Amish entirely. They liked Jonas, and they would support him and their daughter in every way.

Now he just had to get through catechism. Jonas picked up a Bible he'd taken from his parents' home. Sitting down in the secondhand easy chair next to the stove, he opened it and flipped through the pages, looking for John. Finding it, he read the third chapter. He read it again. And again. He had no idea there could be so much in one chapter of the Bible that could apply to him. It talked about being born of water and the Spirit. It talked about living by the truth. It talked about baptism. It said that believing in the Son meant eternal life, but disobeying the Son meant enduring God's wrath.

Jonas had heard plenty about God's wrath from the minis-ters, but he didn't remember hearing anything about God loving the world. Yet there it was, in plain words. And it said that those who believed in God were not condemned.

Jonas leaned back, letting the words soak in and the ques-tions come. Why were people being baptized by John and Jesus? Because they believed. Believed what? Believed that Jesus was the Son of God.

So, is that what his baptism was all about? Believing that Jesus was the Son of God? Was it that simple?

No, it couldn't be. There were weeks of catechism classes to go through. Instruction from the ministers. The passing on of the basics of their beliefs as Amish. But what was the question Debbie had asked after she'd quoted that verse to him?

"Jonas, do you think you're a Christian?"

Was it possible ... could it be that being a Christian and being Amish were two separate things? Of course there were Christians who weren't Amish—Debbie and her family were examples. And what about the other side—were there Amish who weren't Christians? Were there Amish who lived the lifestyle but that was as far as their religion went? That had to be true too.

A strange feeling swept through Jonas. How dare he raise questions like that? Surely God would punish him for those thoughts. The wrath of God ...

And then his eyes fell on the Bible again. "God did not send his Son into the world to condemn the world ... those who believe in him are not condemned...."

Jonas closed his eyes. He'd prayed many times before. That is, he'd repeated words taught to him. Now, for the first time, he spoke to God in his own words.

❖ ❖ ❖

"One last fling before you start joining," Harlan had called it, and Jonas gladly accepted. He loved basketball, so Harlan's offer to take him to a basketball tournament at Vicksburg College during Thanksgiving weekend sounded great. Now, seated in the large, loud arena, they snacked on popcorn and nachos in between games. The fired-up Vicksburg College pep band had the spectators clapping and rocking.

"Debbie almost came to Vicksburg on a music scholarship," Harlan yelled above the noise. "They've got a great music program here."

Jonas nodded, his mouth full of popcorn. He knew Debbie had considered Vicksburg before choosing a private Christian school.

"Whatcha gonna do if one of your kids is really talented— like in music or sports?" Harlan grinned at Jonas, popping a chip dripping with cheese into his mouth. "You might have a star basketball player under your roof, and he'll never get to do anything about it."

"I'm not even married, and you're already worried about my kid being a basketball player?!"

"Just giving you a hard time!" Harlan laughed. "You say you're joining the 'horses' because it's better for your children. I was just wondering what happens if your children are into something the Amish religion doesn't allow, that's all."

"Maybe then you'll have to adopt them," Jonas grinned back.

"Yeah, maybe so," Harlan smiled, scooping the last bit of cheese out of the tray with a tortilla chip. "At least you can have them come work for me, and I'll do my best to corrupt them."

❖ ❖ ❖

Basketball was far from Jonas's mind the next morning as he sat rigidly in one of the upstairs bedrooms of Leon Miller's house. Two ministers, the deacon, and the bishop were there too, all seated in straight-back chairs, all very serious. Jonas desperately wished at least one other young person would be taking catechism with him, but he was alone. His mother had just finished sewing his new black coat, pants, and plain white shirt yesterday. Yes, he was starting to join church.

The bishop began by asking Jonas if he was serious about joining, and if he was ready to take on the discipline of the *Ordnung* in his life. Jonas knew the *Ordnung* was the understood behavior by which Amish are expected to live. An ordering of an entire way of life, the *Ordnung* was something he'd grown up with, rebelled against as a teen, and was now willing to assume for himself as an adult. Jonas nodded yes, he was ready.

Chapter 16

The bishop then went on to explain the importance of baptism and communion as the principal elements of true Christian faith. Jonas listened intently. He was glad he'd read John 3 so many times, but there was so much more to learn.

"We will meet before church for the next five months," the bishop concluded the session. "Then, if you are willing, you will be baptized."

❖ ❖ ❖

The five months flew by for Jonas and Sue Ann. Without telling anyone except their parents and those who would be involved in the wedding, they'd set a wedding date of May 20. There was so much to do in preparation! The living area of their buggy shed needed to be ready for them to move in after their wedding. Clothes had to be sewn—another new suit for Jonas; a new dress, cape, and apron for Sue Ann. Five couples from the young folks were chosen as table waiters, and the girls all needed matching dresses. An Amish woodworker in the community was contacted about making individually crafted gifts for the table waiters and other wedding helpers. Invitations and personalized wedding napkins had to be ordered. And the food—some would come from the canning and freezing the Eashes had done that summer and fall; other items would need to be purchased. The Eash house would get a thorough top-to-bottom cleaning, and the walls freshly painted. Cris decided that, with his new tractors and larger equipment, this was a good time to put up a new Morton building in which to store his machinery. If they pushed it, the building would be ready for the wedding. The service itself could take place in the shed, and the meal in the house. The list of things to do seemed endless, and Jonas was glad Sue Ann appeared to be in control.

The last Sunday in April was Jonas's baptism. He'd completed the five months of instruction. At the last session, the ministers had emphasized over and over the difficulty of walking "the straight and narrow way." "It's better not to make a vow than to make it and later break it," they'd said. "Are you firmly convicted that you are ready to submit to the order of the church?"

As strongly as Jonas knew it was what he wanted to do, a tinge of doubt crept across his mind. What about all of the questions he'd asked in the past? He had to admit, they weren't all answered. But you'll never find all of the answers, he told himself. You'll have to live with the questions, and live within the *Ordnung* at the same time.

And so Jonas found himself kneeling in front of the church, his head bowed low, listening as the bishop asked: "Can you confess with the eunuch 'I believe that Jesus Christ is the Son of God'?"

"Yes, I believe that Jesus Christ is the Son of God," Jonas said.

"Do you also confess this to be a Christian doctrine, church, and brotherhood to which you are about to submit?"

"Yes."

"Do you now renounce the world, the devil, and his evil lusts, as well as your own flesh and blood, and desire to serve only Jesus Christ, who died on the cross for you?"

"Yes," Jonas said, emotion welling up inside his heart. He remembered reading the Bible that evening last November. He remembered the forgiveness and assurance he felt as he prayed to God in his own words. Something had happened to him then, something that he was publicly declaring now. He heard the bishop's last question.

"Do you also promise, in the presence of God and the church, with the Lord's help to support these doctrines and regulations, to earnestly fill your place in the church, to help counsel and labor, and not depart from the same, come what may, life or death?"

"Yes."

The congregation was standing for prayer as Jonas remained on his knees. Soon he felt the bishop's hands on his head, and then water being poured through the cupped hands. "God, wash me whiter than snow," he prayed from his soul as the water dripped off his head. "Help me to remain faithful!"

The bishop was extending his hand toward Jonas. Jonas reached for it and stood up as the bishop intoned, "In the name of the Lord and the church, I offer you my hand. Please rise." He then greeted Jonas with a "holy kiss" and wished him peace.

Jonas sat down on the backless bench as the church service continued. For some strange reason, he thought of Enos. Enos, his best friend who'd been killed before he was baptized. Tears that didn't come the day Enos died nearly five years earlier now welled up in Jonas's eyes.

Chapter 17

Hitched

"It's good to see you again, Naomi," Jonas greeted Sue Ann's cousin from Missouri the evening of May 19 as she stood in the Eash kitchen, peeling carrots. "We appreciate your being willing to be a table waiter."

"Thanks for asking me," the cute freckle-faced teenager replied. "I'm really happy for both of you."

"Now if you can just keep Edwin in line, we'll all be happy," Jonas joked, nudging the young man cutting up celery next to Naomi. "We hoped if we matched you two up as table waiters, your sensibleness would balance his craziness."

"I'll do my best," Naomi replied, glancing up at Edwin. "And I'll try to keep him off the ropes in the barn."

"Hey, I won't be doin' any swingin' this time," Edwin drawled slowly. "At least not from ropes. Right, guys?" he addressed the four other young men in the kitchen, all of them busy working with food for the next day. Standing next to the male table waiters were their female partners, also occupied with food preparation.

"Right! We've got other things planned!" one of the table waiters laughed. "Makes rope swingin' look tame, man, tame!"

"You guys behave yourselves," Sue Ann admonished. "I'm trusting you with four of my best friends, not to mention my soon-to-be sister-in-law!"

"Oh, we girls can take care of ourselves," Roseanne replied. "Don't worry about us."

Jonas and Sue Ann exchanged glances. They'd both been table waiters at other weddings. They knew how much fun—usually "good, clean fun"—the table waiters had together. They also knew that occasionally the fun got out of hand.

"Actually, what I'm more worried about is the weather," Sue Ann looked through the window over the kitchen sink. "It's looking nasty."

"The radio in the van said there's a real good chance of rain tonight," Naomi contributed.

"What about tomorrow?" Jonas wondered.

"I don't remember."

"Well, we're gettin married rain or shine!" Jonas declared.

"The man is *anxious* to get hitched!" Edwin teased. "Say good-bye to your freedom!"

"Oh no, I'm sayin hello to *livin*'!" Jonas winked larger-than-life and drew Sue Ann close to him.

Sue Ann's blush didn't go unnoticed by the young folks who paused in their peeling and cutting long enough to glance at the bride-to-be.

"Now if you can just get that man of yours to build you a house before you fill that buggy shed with children," Edwin continued the joshing.

"You know, we don't have to put up with this," Jonas took Sue Ann's hand and began to walk out of the kitchen. "I bet there're some relatives from out-of-state showing up at my folks that we need to go see. See you all later!"

Jonas and Sue Ann climbed into the borrowed buggy and clucked at Lightning to head out.

"Good thing we have the new buggy for tomorrow," Jonas said, referring to their wedding gift from his parents. "It's in the shed staying clean, while this one will probably get muddy before tonight's over."

"Everything will be a mess if it's muddy tomorrow," Sue Ann said.

A clap of thunder crashed around them, and Lightning jumped. Sue Ann moved even closer to Jonas and put her arm through his. Suddenly it began to pour.

Please, God, Jonas prayed silently, let it be nice tomorrow.

It was after midnight by the time Jonas took Sue Ann home and then went to stay with Lyndon, his cousin and best man. The Bontrager home was full of family guests, so it made sense for Jonas to spend what was left of the night at his aunt and uncle's house.

Jonas heard the storm off and on during the short night, and by 5:00 he was on his way back to the Eash farm. He didn't feel rested, but adrenaline had replaced sleep. In fact, he almost felt like he could run to the Eashes faster than Lightning was going. Poor horse hasn't had much of a night either, Jonas realized.

Turning Lightning into the Eash yard, Jonas smiled, seeing the house was already lit up. The cooks were at it bright and early, preparing the massive meal that would serve more than 300 guests. There would be turkey and dressing, chicken, mashed potatoes and gravy, corn, Jell-O, tossed salad, tapioca salad, homemade bread, and cinnamon rolls. And then, Jonas remembered from other weddings, when a person was so full he couldn't move, the table waiters would bring out the pies and cakes— three or four kinds of fruit pies, a sheet cake, and angel food cake.

Jonas realized he hadn't had any breakfast, and the smells coming out of the house were about to drive him crazy. He unhitched Lightning and led him into the large red barn. Even the barn had received a thorough cleaning for the occasion; by 9:30 it would house around 40 horses. Another 60 would spend their day tied up side by side in the hay shed.

"Well, big guy," Jonas patted Lightning on the neck as he tied him up in one of the stalls, "Next time we see each other, you'll be pulling the buggy of married folks!"

Jonas stepped out of the barn and noticed a lantern light in the large metal building where the wedding service would be held. He'd helped set up the rows and rows of backless church benches the day before, so everything should be in order. He walked toward the shed.

"Morning!" Cris greeted him as he stepped inside the large sliding doors. "I was just looking it all over again, seeing if we forgot anything. Couldn't stay in the house—I'm just in the way there!"

"Yeah, I bet," Jonas agreed.

"Soon as it gets light enough, I think we'll see if there're places on the yard that need sand or boards put over the mud and water," Cris said.

The windmill near the horse barn groaned and creaked. Jonas and Cris watched as the metal blade slowly swung around and the large wheel started spinning.

"Wind's turned to the north," Cris stated. "Rain's over."

More than ever in his life, Jonas hoped the Amish "weather wisdom" would hold true. He looked east at the horizon. Clouds covered any chance of seeing the sunrise.

Despite the overcast sky, it wasn't long until there was enough light to see the yard and the areas where several shovels of sand or some boards would help people navigate the mud and water spots. Jonas and Cris went to work.

Jonas was bending down, laying a plank of wood for a walkway into the shed, when suddenly a stream of sunlight struck his eyes. Jonas squinted into the unexpected invasion. High above him, as if pushed by a mighty hand sweeping its way across the sky, the clouds were scurrying away. A strange thought crossed Jonas's mind as he watched. The clouds almost looked guilty. As if sorry for the mess they'd left, and now ... now they were muttering, "We're outta here!"

Jonas swallowed hard, and his eyes suddenly filled. Maybe, like Cris said, it was the north wind. Maybe, just maybe, God answered prayers.

❖ ❖ ❖

By 9:00, as a steady stream of buggies rolled into the Eash yard, an absolutely perfect spring morning was in process. After chasing the clouds away, the wind had calmed down to a soft breeze. Full, bright sunshine smiled on the freshly watered world—a world that responded with uplifted flower faces and top-of-the-lungs chorusing birds. The gathering family, friends, and neighbors commented again and again on the beautiful morning as they made their way to the red shed.

Chapter 17

Around 9:30, everyone was seated except the cooks, Jonas, Sue Ann, and their attendants. Without any fanfare or music, Lyndon and Sue Ann's sister Lydi led the small procession to the front, followed by Jonas and Sue Ann, then Roseanne and her partner. They sat in two rows of chairs facing each other, guys in one row, girls in the other.

Without a doubt, Jonas heard the ministers preach on marriage that morning in their singsong voices. But occasionally, his eyes and thoughts strayed. He noticed that Harlan, Lynne and Debbie had accepted their invitation to attend, and he was glad to see them there. And more than once he found himself losing concentration, absorbed in the young woman across from him.

Does she know how much I love her? he wondered. Does she understand how beautiful she is, inside and out? He smiled slightly, and Sue Ann's lips parted briefly in response.

I'll never forget how she looks today in her blue dress, starched white cape, apron, and covering, Jonas told himself. If we weren't Amish, we'd have pictures of us today, but now it'll just be our memories. Unless, of course, one of the table waiters or other young folks snaps a picture or two, he smiled again.

Around 11:00, during one of the minister's talks, a row of about ten women filed into the shed. The cooks had left their food preparation to get in on the vows. Jonas shifted his position slightly and his heart quickened. It was getting closer now.

Finally the bishop stood up and began talking. After what seemed like a long time, he asked Jonas and Sue Ann to stand and face him.

Jonas stood, his palms nervously hanging at his side. The

bishop addressed the two of them. "Do you believe and confess that so as to have a Christian order and union there shall be one man and one wife, and do you both feel that you have started this preparation for marriage in a way that you have been taught?"

"Yes," Jonas and Sue Ann responded.

"Do you feel, brother, that God has brought this sister to you to behold and take as your wife?"

"Yes," Jonas said. The bishop repeated the question to Sue Ann, and Jonas thrilled to hear her "yes."

"Do you, brother, promise your wife that if she should fall into sorrow, grief, or pain, weakness of body or sickness of any kind, that you will share it with her and care for her as a Christian man should?"

Jonas's "yes" was followed by the same question to Sue Ann and her affirmative response. Then the bishop spoke to them both again. "Do you both promise each other that you will love and cherish each other, be patient, gentle and kind to each other and not part from each other until our loving God shall part you through death?"

"Yes," they replied.

The bishop asked the congregation to stand, and led in a prayer, asking for God's blessing on Jonas and Sue Ann. After the prayer and the congregation was seated again, the bishop took Sue Ann's hand and placed it in Jonas's hand. Jonas had held her hand many times, but this was different. This was a holy moment. Through the emotions swelling within him, Jonas heard the bishop declare, "In the name of our Lord and the church I hereby pronounce you man and wife, and may God's blessings rest upon you and keep you till death doth thee part, and all this in the name of our Lord Jesus Christ. You may now take your seats again. You are no longer two, but one flesh and spirit with God. Amen."

Jonas wiped his clammy hands on his pants and took a deep breath as they sat down and the congregation began the final hymn. He caught Sue Ann's glistening eyes and held them for a moment with his own. The somber affirmation he'd repeated reverberated in his heart until he felt it could explode. YES! YES! YES!

❖ ❖ ❖

Serving a huge meal to over 300 people in their home would daunt most "English" couples, but the Amish handled the challenge with experience and efficiency. Tables and benches had been set up the day before in every available room in the house— enough to seat 150 people in one sitting. Following the service, the guests began filling the house, and the table waiters went to work. The five young couples may have had plans for fun and craziness later, but for the moment, they were working hard.

Jonas, Sue Ann, and their attendants found their way to "The Corner." This section of the table, traditionally set up in a corner of the living or dining room, was the focus of much interest and attention, as it featured the beautifully decorated wedding cake. Unique gifts to the bride and groom could often be found there, as well as certain foods that only those in "The Corner" were privileged to get. Jonas noticed a jar of cherry tomatoes next to his plate.

"Tomatoes?" he asked Sue Ann, who just laughed and said, "Beats me!"

"Anybody want to explain the tomatoes?" Jonas asked, noticing that Lydi could hardly keep a straight face.

"Thought you might need some, after you wasted so many on Sue Ann's window," she giggled.

"Oh, okay. Well, you have to admit, I've got pretty good aim," Jonas took a tomato out of the jar and pretended to aim for Lydi.

"Nope, better not," he added. "I'm a responsible married man now!"

"Ha!" Lyndon guffawed.

"So what's with the big bag of sunflower seeds here in the corner?" Sue Ann queried. "Lyndon?"

"Don't look at me!"

A tinkling noise started in one part of the room and soon spread throughout the tables of guests. Jonas blushed, knowing he and Sue Ann would need to obey the demand of the utensils tapping against water glasses. He leaned over and kissed her on the cheek.

The verbal protests and incessant tinkling that followed made their point. Jonas and Sue Ann kissed again, their mouths touching softly. This time the onlookers were appeased, at least for the moment.

Jonas, Sue Ann, and their attendants stayed in The Corner through the feeding of the second shift of people—laughing, joking, and greeting the guests. Once when Jonas happened to look out the window, he nudged Sue Ann and nodded in the direction of the barn.

Their shiny, new, black buggy stood outside the barn doors, surrounded by "decorators" and "cheerleaders." Toilet paper adorned the wheels, and more was in process.

"I think we'll need to take it for a ride later," Jonas said.

"Definitely! As long as we're back in plenty of time for supper and the singing," Sue Ann agreed.

The afternoon passed quickly as adults visited, children played, and the young folks hung around a group of buggies where music and liquid refreshments kept them entertained. Late in the afternoon, Jonas asked Lyndon to bring Lightning out of the barn. Together, they hitched him up to the decorated buggy.

"Now, one more thing," Jonas said to Lyndon. "Could you bring that bag of sunflower seeds out here?"

Lyndon threw him a quizzical look but dutifully sauntered toward the house. Jonas laughed to himself, then turned to some girls nearby.

"Sue Ann *Bontrager!*" he called. "Would you like to go for a ride?"

"Yes, I'd love to!" she walked to the buggy. "And would you be *Mr.* Bontrager?"

"I am," Jonas said, giving her his hand as she stepped up into the buggy.

"And where might we be going?"

"Well, let's see," Jonas said, looking down at Lyndon, who stood next to the buggy with the large bag of sunflower seeds. Then he turned to Sue Ann. "Could you open your hankie, please?"

Mystified, Sue Ann withdrew a white handkerchief from the waistline of her apron. She unfolded the gift from her grandmother and laid it on her lap.

"Now, Lyndon, hand me a dozen of those seeds," Jonas instructed.

Jonas took the seeds and dropped them carefully onto the delicate handkerchief. "Now you can tie it shut," he said quietly. "You know where we're going, don't you?"

Sue Ann smiled into Jonas's eyes, and he melted into hers. For a moment, they connected in a world of their own. Finally, Jonas broke the spell. Glancing at the curious people gathered around the buggy, he took Lightning's reins in his hands.

"We'll be back," he told the crowd. "But first, we've got some sunflower seeds to plant!"

❖ ❖ ❖

Jonas stood up from where he'd been kneeling in the freshly spaded dirt in front of the buggy wheel. Several days earlier, he'd dug the wheel into the ground near a cottonwood stump on his yard. Then he'd created a flower bed around the wheel and tree stump, and now the first seeds were in the ground.

"It'll look nice with the tall sunflowers in the background, and some marigolds in front," Sue Ann noted as she stood beside Jonas and reached for his hand.

"Yeah," Jonas responded. "It's a beginning. I want this to be a beautiful place. For you, for us, for our kids." He paused as he drew Sue Ann closer to him. "I still can't believe how lucky I am to be married to you." His eyes traveled from the small flower bed to the remains of the stately cottonwood grove. "And sometimes it's almost scary. Like today is too good to be true, and we don't know what our future holds for us. You know what I mean?"

Sue Ann turned to meet her husband's clear blue eyes. "Kind of like 'The Dance'? We've had some pain already, but today we get to dance," she stopped, and a slow smile inched its way across her face. "Oh yeah, I forgot, Amish don't dance. Well, knowing you and your questioning, you'll push the issue. And I'm happy to be your partner."

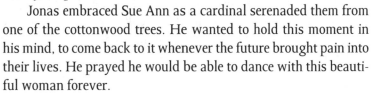

137

Chapter
17

Jonas embraced Sue Ann as a cardinal serenaded them from one of the cottonwood trees. He wanted to hold this moment in his mind, to come back to it whenever the future brought pain into their lives. He prayed he would be able to dance with this beautiful woman forever.

THE END

Coming Next:
Preacher
Book 3 ❖ Jonas Series

The Authors

Husband-and-wife authors Maynard Knepp and Carol Duerksen share their farm between Goessel and Hillsboro, Kansas, with exchange students and a variety of animals. Maynard grew up Amish near Yoder, Kansas, and provided the inspiration and information for this book. Carol is a full-time freelance writer. They are active members of the Tabor Mennonite Church.

The Illustrator

Susan Bartel has illustrated several books and many magazine stories. She lives with her husband and two children at Rocky Mountain Mennonite Camp near Divide, Colorado.

OTHER BOOKS FROM
WILLOWSPRING DOWNS

JONAS SERIES

The Jonas Series was the brainchild of Maynard Knepp, a popular speaker on the Amish culture who grew up in an Amish family in central Kansas. Knepp and his wife Carol Duerksen, a freelance writer, collaborated to produce their first book, *Runaway Buggy*, released in October, 1995. The resounding success of that book encouraged them to continue, and the series grew to four books within 18 months. The books portray the Amish as real people who face many of the same decisions, joys and sorrows as everyone else, as well as those that are unique to their culture and tradition. Written in an easy-to-read style that appeals to a wide range of ages and diverse reader base — from elementary age children to folks in their 90s, from dairy farmers to PhDs — fans of the Jonas Series are calling it captivating, intriguing, can't-put-it-down reading.

RUNAWAY BUGGY

This book sweeps the reader into the world of an Amish youth trying to find his way "home." Not only does *Runaway Buggy* pull back a curtain to more clearly see a group of people, but it intimately reveals the heart of one of their sons struggling to become a young man all his own.

HITCHED

With *Hitched*, the second installment in the Jonas Series, the reader struggles with Jonas as he searches for the meaning of Christianity and tradition, and feels his bewilderment as he recognizes that just as there are Christians who are not Amish, there are Amish who are not Christians.

PREACHER

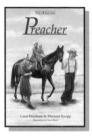

Book Three in the Jonas Series finds Jonas Bontrager the owner of a racehorse named Preacher, and facing dilemmas that only his faith can explain, and only his faith can help him endure.

BECCA

The fourth book in the Jonas Series invites readers to see the world through the eyes of Jonas Bontrager's 16-year-old daughter Becca, as she asks the same questions her father did, but in her own fresh and surprising ways.

SKYE SERIES

A spin-off of the much-loved Jonas Series, the Skye Series follows Jonas Bontrager's daughter Becca as she marries and becomes the mother of twin daughters, Angela and Skye. While Angela rests on an inner security of who she is and what life is about, Skye's journey takes her to very different places and situations. Through it all, she holds tightly to one small red piece of security—a bandanna her Amish grandfather gave her as a child.

TWINS

In the first book of the Skye Series, Becca and her husband Ken become the parents of twin daughters through very unusual circumstances—circumstances that weave the twins' lives together even as they are pulled apart by their separate destinies.

AFFAIR OF THE HEART

Not long after rock star Skye Martin settles into the Wellsford Amish community, the tongues begin to wag. She's been seen a lot lately with Ezra Yoder, an Amish man who always did seem to have secrets of his own.

Slickfester Dude
Tells Bedtime Stories
Life Lessons from our Animal Friends

by Carol Duerksen (& Slickfester Dude)

WillowSpring Downs is not only a publishing company — it's also a 120-acre piece of paradise in central Kansas that's home to a wide assortment of animals. Slickfester Dude, a black cat with three legs that work and one that doesn't, is one of those special animals. In a unique book that only a very observant cat could write, Slickfester Dude tells Carol a bedtime story every night — a story of life among the animals and what it can mean for everyone's daily life. This book will delight people from elementary age and up because the short stories are told in words that both children and adults can understand and take to heart. Along with strong, sensitive black and white story illustrations, the book includes Slickfester Dude's Photo Album of his people and animal friends at WillowSpring Downs.

VISIT OUR WEB SITES:

http://www.geocities.com/Eureka/Plaza/1638
http://www.geocities.com/Heartland/Ranch/7719

ORDER FORM

Jonas Series: *($9.95 each **OR** 2 or more, any title mix, $10 each, we pay shipping.)*

_____ copy/copies of *Runaway Buggy*

_____ copy/copies of *Hitched*

_____ copy/copies of *Preacher*

_____ copy/copies of *Becca*

_____ Jonas Series—all 4 books, $36.50

> For more information
> or to be added to our
> mailing list,
> call or fax us on our
> toll-free number
> **1-888-551-0973**

Skye Series:

_____ copy/copies of *Twins* @ $9.95 each

_____ copy/copies of *Affair of the Heart* @ $9.95 each

Other:

_____ copy/copies of *Slickfester Dude Tells Bedtime Stories* @ $9.95 each

Name _____

Address _____

City _____ State _____

Zip _____ Phone # _____

_____ Book(s) at $9.95 = Total $ _____

Add $3 postage/handling if only one copy _____

**SPECIAL PRICE = Buy 2 or more,
pay $10 each and we'll pay the shipping.**

Total enclosed $ _____

Make checks payable to WillowSpring Downs and mail, along with this order form, to the following address:

**WillowSpring Downs
1582 N. Falcon
Hillsboro, KS 67063-9600**